We are each our own devil, and we make this world our hell.
Oscar Wilde

Disclaimer

The stories in this book are fiction. This book is not a substitute for health care, medication, or any treatment not specified. The author does not assume any responsibility or legal liability if an individual uses information in this book and experiences abnormal or detrimental psychological, physical, or medical effects, or any consequence not mentioned. It is always a good idea to speak with a doctor before changing a health care routine.

Through the Gates of Hell
Stories of Caffeine Psychosis

There's a fine line between sanity and madness, and millions of people do not know they crossed over. Millions exist in a living purgatory, between heaven and hell, unaware their psyche swings between truth and fantasy, good and evil, will and want...

Ruth Whalen
Photography By
Mike Dijital

For my daughter, with love

The mind is its own place, and in itself can
make a heaven of hell, a hell of heaven.
John Milton

Danvers State Hospital, Danvers, Massachusetts, Circa 1908

Preface

Albert Einstein claimed, "The only source of knowledge is experience." A medical professional, I verify that. Misdiagnosed for over twenty-four years, I recovered from caffeine psychosis after a good doctor diagnosed me with an allergy to caffeine. I came forward to inform the public that caffeine-induced illness is commonly diagnosed as ADHD, schizophrenia, bipolar disorder, panic, OCD, depression, and other made-up disorders. I knew my findings might upset many people, and I believed many people would reject my findings. In fact, someone posted negative comments about my work and writing skills online. Sometimes that's how it goes, but the truth isn't always easy to hide. Numerous people erroneously diagnosed with ADHD, anxiety, or mental illness read my work and recovered from psychosis. The individuals reclaimed their health and threw away their psychiatric drugs. As for my writing skills? Everyone is entitled to an opinion.

Several health care professionals suggested that I write this book. They encouraged me to entertain while educating readers about the dangers of caffeine.

This book is primarily fiction. The names of all persons in this book are made-up. Any resemblance to a known person is strictly coincidence, and except for a bit of information about the Boston Tea Party, the stories are fiction, dark fiction.

The book may disturb some people, but we don't live in a candy cane world. With the absurd availability of psychiatric drugs, cola, coffee, and bottled water containing caffeine, the good, old days are far behind us.

Many people deserve recognition for believing in me and helping to bring this information to the public. First, I thank the man who contributed to this book. A gifted photographer, Mike Dijital dedicated his heart and soul to our project, staying on board from the beginning. Thank you very much, Mike.

I thank my daughter for inspiring me. My daughter went through hell because doctors misdiagnosed me, and I continued ingesting caffeine not knowing I am allergic to the legal psychoactive drug. I cannot change the past, but I will continue to inform the public about the dangers of caffeine, modern medicine, and psychiatry because every child deserves a peaceful childhood and every person deserves to be healthy.

My friends are terrific individuals. I thank Charles, Hambone, Jim,

Richard, Monica, Deborah, Chris, Donna, Kris, Joan, Paula, Ricky, Sarah, Mindy, Georgia, Susi, Dave, Bob, and Patricia for supporting my efforts and encouraging me. I thank my attorney friend, Ted Schwartz, for encouraging me and reviewing my work. Let's keep laughing, ladies and gentlemen. That's what life is about.

Andrew Saul, Ph.D. and Abram Hoffer, M.D., Ph.D., FRCP (C), I am grateful that you acknowledged my work and published my articles. Thank you for everything.

I thank the four individuals who came forward and shared their experiences in *Medical Veritas*, the journal of medical truth.

I thank J.M. Sawyer for donating photographs to this project. Also, I thank Paul Anderson, Jason Baker, Blackwood Associates, Inc., Architects and Planners, Marlon Paul Bruin, Michael Connors, M. van den Dobbelsteen, J.R. Goleno, Allan Kilgour, Keith Manfredi, James Maskrey, Troy Newell, and Stewart Whitmore for contributing photos.

Tom Cruise, thank you for your support and encouraging words. Tom's opinion about "mental illness" hit a bull's eye.

It's time my daughter and I head to Ireland, where we can peddle bicycles, sit in the pubs, laugh, write, and enjoy our fill of Scotch whiskey. We'll bring my wallet and our sense of humors.

Through the Gates of Hell
Stories of Caffeine Psychosis

Contents

Introduction	11
1. A Dollar's Worth	13
2. Into Hell	16
3. All the King's Horses	19
4. Leon's Misfortune	24
5. Homeward Bound	27
6. In the Web	32
7. Simon	37
8. Strike Three	40
9. Ruben's Journal	48
10. Hail Mary	52
11. The Forrester House	57
12. Shades of Gray	61
13. The Number Nine	66
14. Only Dreams	70
15. The Interrogation	75
16. Johnny's Red Wagon	78
17. The Green Café	81
18. Flipside	88
19. Can't Blame it on the Cow	94
20. Sunny Daze	97
21. Top O' the Morning	100
22. Me Too	102
23. Eleventh Grade Chemistry	105
24. Flowers for All Occasions	110
25. Three Tickets Free	116
26. Inclement Weather	120
27. Selective Serotonin Reuptake Instigators	127

Introduction

There's a fine line between sanity and madness, and millions of people do not know they crossed over. Millions of people exist in a living purgatory, between heaven and hell, unaware that their psyche swings between truth and fantasy, good and evil, will and want.

Wandering in the gloaming, trying to come home, shackled with anxiety, restlessness, fever, headaches, paranoia, mood swings, tears, guilt, frustration, discouragement, hallucinations, voices, nightmares and more, little and small, young and old, black, brown, white and yellow are driven to despair. Crippled emotionally, infants sucking tea-tainted breast milk never obtain a chance to sip life. Ingesting chocolate pudding and chocolate milk, children gated in playpens are chained to a future of attention deficits, obsession, paranoia, psychiatric drugs and more. School children fidget in their seats, listening to voices in their heads tell them to settle down, mothers fixing breakfast are lost in the hours of teacup delusions, and men running from insanity ask, "Why?" Self-erased, the elderly are carted to nursing homes, given a room, and a number, lost amidst their faulty chemistry, without memories. Misplaced souls walk aimlessly from one hour to the next. Patients linger on deathbeds, obsessing about their lives, regrets, and sickness. And people swallowing psychiatric medications to eradicate players, demons of their minds, ask, "Why me?" and "How did this happen?"

Stuck in an apocalypse, minds cast thoughts of dark and light, with the brain altered by an everyday poison. And as the altered self deteriorates in its progressive physical and mental frenzy, individuals race from doctor to doctor, therapist to psychiatrist, from the emergency room to the pharmacy, asking, "Why?" They mumble, "There's no mental illness in my family" and "I can't live like this." Patients beg, "Please, help me!" And *physically ill* patients go home and take *psychiatric drugs* with the very substance that caused their physical and mental demise, and they never recover.

Countless people don't realize they are straddling another side. They lost the ability to realize, and only a handful of people know to think back, back to when they did not ingest caffeine.

Drinking coffee and cola, and snacking on chocolate, people lose focus, their intellect deteriorates, and they blame mental illness, Parkinson's disease, Alzheimer's, cancer and more on genetics, childhood, mothers, fathers, and more, because they cannot see the picture when they are standing in the frame, but the world is not flat.

Physicians and psychiatrists tarred the road of destruction, helping to destroy the very lives they were to save, introducing a dam of absurdities into society, enabling it to burst into a sea of atrocities, accepted by millions of caffeine users.

Unknown to most people, caffeine inhibits monoamine oxidase (1-3), an enzyme necessary to break down adrenaline, natural speed. Consequently, caffeine increases adrenaline (2, 3). Caffeine also increases acetylcholine and serotonin (2, 3). And doctors should be ashamed of themselves for diagnosing caffeine users with ADHD, mental disorders, Parkinson's disease, Alzheimer's dementia, other phony conditions and prescribing SSRI drugs to patients that ingest caffeine.

Caffeine causes many other biochemical imbalances (2, 3), discussed in *Welcome to the Dance: Caffeine Allergy, A Masked Cerebral Allergy and Progressive Toxic Dementia*, the first documented discussion about caffeine psychosis, caffeine allergy and endogenous toxicity, so-called mental illness. I wrote the book because countless cases of so-called ADHD, anxiety, and mental illness result from the everyday poison in almost every person's kitchen, a nerve tonic and pesticide ingested by the multitude (2, 3). I wrote the book because abnormal blood test results mean that a person is in an abnormal physical state, and countless psychiatric patients have abnormal blood test results (2, 3).

Joe, java, call it what you will, caffeine rules heads, rapes souls, and pushes its victims onto the highway of preventable insanity, violence, suicide (2,4) and death—But because caffeine acts like amphetamine, caffeine users do not know they are "high" (2, 4).

On with the show. No more references. Caffeine psychosis isn't a black-tie affair.

References:
1. Hoffer A & Osmond H. The Hallucinogens. New York: Academic Press, 1967.
2. Whalen R. Foreword by Hoffer A. Welcome to the Dance: Caffeine Allergy, A Masked Cerebral Allergy and Progressive Toxic Dementia. Victoria; Trafford, 2005-2006.
3. Whalen R. Ongoing caffeine anaphylaxis: a differential for mental illness. Medical Veritas 2004; 1(2): 252-260.
4. Elkins F, Farver D, Rolim IL, Janisch G. Medical Veritas. Caffeine allergy forum 2004; 1(2): 315-319.

1
A Dollar's Worth

Photo by Keith Manfredi

"Step right up! A nickel a guess! You win, I lose, seven cents back! Step right up!" Anastasia barked. Her clear, green eyes stalked the crowd, searching for a loser. A nickel a try was a small price to learn the truth from an old woman in a red cotton dress, hanging to her ankles.

"Step right up! Take a seat! Anastasia knows what you've had to eat!"

Anastasia targeted an overweight man eating a Cadoo chocolate bar. Staggering, he appeared drunk. "You! If I guess and lose, you win seven cents!" Ignoring the peculiar woman, the stranger ambled past the wooden booth. "Keep going like you are—and you'll be dead before your time. Not a dime! Only a nickel!"

Her forehead dampened from the balmy evening, Ivy tugged her mother's bare arm. "Momma, can I try? Please, please!"

"That's it, little one. Hop onto Anastasia's magic stool."

One after the other, Ivy's feet banged the wooden stool. Running two fingers along the child's arm, Anastasia felt dryness. "You don't like water." Smiling, the frail brunette shook her head. "And you don't like carrots or lettuce. Am I right?"

"My, my," the mother said, advancing. "What else do you know?"

Anastasia felt the child's pulse. *Racing like a cat after rabbit meat.* "Tonic. She drank Captain Kid Cola." *Flakes in her hair. Cracker crumbs on her sleeves? Maybe bread.* "And the youngster ate a sandwich for dinner, before you rushed to the carnival. Am I right?" The mother held out a nickel.

"Step right up!" Shouting at a thin woman wearing maroon pedal pushers and a white blouse, Anastasia kept it up. "You, over there. Only a nickel to learn the truth! I'm living proof!"

"Do it, Mom!"

"Shhh, Morris. I can't afford it."

Theresa's fifteen-year-old son pulled a dime from his loafer. "Do it," he urged.

Beckoning Theresa and her ducklings to the booth, Anastasia reminded, "It's only a nickel, not a dime."

The old woman slowly pushed up a sleeve. It scraped the eczema-covered arm. "No water for you. No salmon, cod, or flounder either."

Focused on Theresa's glassy eyes, Anastasia claimed she liked coffee. "And you drink a lot. Had your fill today, didn't you?"

"How does she know?" Sadie whispered.

Hooking her sister's arm, Dorrie called Anastasia a witch.

"A 'witch' you say?" Clear eyes darted from one child to the next. "Captain Kid Cola. You all drink the demon cola!" Backing away from the boisterous woman, the children trembled. "That's it! Run scared from Anastasia. I know the truth!"

Barking, Anastasia watched two policemen push a stretcher through the crowd. Anxious to see what was going on, onlookers scattered.

Anastasia silently cursed, elbowing her way through the crowd: *Damn Cadoos, Captain Kid, coffee and tea. They get 'em every time.* Slumped over a picnic table, the obese man moaned in pain.

"Rusty, he was eating a chocolate bar when he passed me," Anastasia informed. "Must be loaded with the poison."

"Get him some water, boys!" Rusty, the manager, yelled.

"Anastasia, you amaze me." Hoisting the man onto the stretcher, Officer O'Brien asked, "How do you know what you know?"

"In 1889, I buried my father. 'Exhaustion,' Doc Smith claimed.

'How can that be?' I asked, sixteen, witness to my thirty-eight-year-old father drinking coffee and lounging in the sun most his days. Telling me it was common, Dr. Smith patted my shoulder."

Scratching his chin, Officer O'Brien asked if Anastasia knew what happened.

"Not right away, but one day my sister dropped to the floor after morning tea. 'Stress,' Dr. Partridge said. I wasn't convinced.

'Carey's only forty years old,' I reminded him, cradling her lifeless body. Then I spotted the empty cups on the plant stand.

'Must run in the family,' Dr. Partridge stated, pulling the sheet over Carey's head. 'I understand your father died young, too.'

'It has to be the tea,' I insisted, but the doctor ignored me. 'It's the tea!' I smashed the cups on the floor.

Old Partridge wanted me admitted to the state place, but my Kevin disagreed. My husband has faith in me."

"Are you saying the tea killed her?"

"It doesn't take much common sense. Look around." Anastasia pointed to the beverage booth, and then the sweet stand. "Here we are: 1958. You see them wetting their eyes, drying their skin, thoughts racing, lost, murdering. I could go on and on, but for what? Caffeine lovers listen, but they can't process. Their minds obviously lost focus, they forfeited control, and they believe in schizophrenia and manic-depression. Goodness, OB, the world's going to hell in a basket."

Covering the ill man with a thin blanket, Officer O'Brien asked if Anastasia used caffeine.

"I haven't touched it since 1889."

O'Brien stepped back. "'1889'? Good gracious, are you that old?"

"I'll be eighty-six," Anastasia whispered. "It's a secret to most, even Kevin. We just celebrated his seventy-ninth birthday. Life is good."

Looking at the bright stars twinkling above her summer serenity, Anastasia sighed. "A nickel a guess! You win, I lose, seven cents back! Step right up! You think I can't tell? You all passed through the gates of hell!"

2
Into Hell

Photo by M van den Dobbelsteen

Gathered in The Boston Pub and the Yankee Coffee House, and centered in Charlestown and surrounding town squares, protestors discussed the voice of the people, rejection of tea from London's Tea Company. Thirty miles north of Boston, at a meeting with his peers, in a Protestant church, Governor Dennison adhered to his agenda. "The tea will arrive in Massachusetts," Dennison stated, "and the people will pay tax on it!"

They didn't want it. Happy with their personal affairs, mill workers, blacksmiths, fishermen, traders and other workers rallied, but to no avail. Five British ships transporting tea and Dennison's nephews, tea agents, arrived in Boston Harbor, at Daybreak Wharf.

Ninety men, a rough count, faces and hands painted vermilion, carried tomahawks and rifles along Boston's streets. Challenging the misty evening, the patriots were determined to turn the ships around, to force the journey back to London.

As supporters crowded the wharf, the men climbed aboard the vessels. On the decks, wooden crates sat atop one another, patiently waiting their destruction. As planned, the men lashed open crates, more than 400, direct from London, allowing black tea to spill upon the ships and into frigid water.

"No tea!" a witness to the ravage cried.

The crowd joined him. "No tea! No tea, no tea!" the cold air seemed to howl.

As several loyalists fired guns, others savagely hoisted crates and dumped tea into the harbor. A handful of witnesses excitedly rushed into the low tide and waded through muck to catch a feel of the despised tea. Peasants filled their wool caps and pockets with the wet, salted tea.

"No salted tea!" a carriage driver hollered, pointing at the thieves.

Without warning, a fisherman jumped from the dock and pushed a man's head under water. "The thief is drowning!" a woman screamed, turning from the scene.

The night was one to remember, for Bostonians swept the foreign ships unclean, bloodied their own waters and reinforced patriotism and hatred. And yet, not one participant considered that dumping tea into the harbor and the chaos resulting from it could change the course of mental stability and health care, and not for the better, for the darkest worst.

Before the Tea Party, men entered the Yankee Coffee House and ordered tea from Frank Carlisle. After the event, Frank asked, "What'll it be?" Instead of hearing "Tea," Frank heard "Coffee." Sensing defeat, many tea boycotters had switched to drinking coffee.

"It's a small winning," Malloy Ferguson stated, toasting Rufus Patterson in Frank's coffee shop.

"Indeed, it is." Rufus waved at Frank, standing at the counter. "I'll have another coffee!"

And so it was that coffee drinking surpassed tea sipping and became an American popularity. The wealthy established additional coffee houses and, before long, men took to frequenting the gathering places after work, after dinner, and on weekends. But Aesop had the right idea. More than tea, coffee stimulates and causes anxiety, similar to the rushed state of the restless hare. And we all know the tortoise won the race.

Long before the 20th century, medical doctors, solely responsible for listening to health complaints, treated patients. After the Boston Tea Party, doctors referred to certain symptoms of adrenaline toxicity, brought on by stress and caffeine, as psychosomatic, caused by the mind—symptoms brought on by the power of suggestion—a ludicrous assumption.

The official Separation of Mind and Body Era, when many doctors believed the mind separate from the body, spanned the years 1811-1875, after the Tea Party. And symptoms of what doctors know as schizophrenia and bipolar disorder were described after the Tea Party. Were early psychiatrists drinking coffee when they came up with their theories? We shouldn't condemn dead men, but they seemed to have damned society. At any rate, with ongoing complaints, doctors unable to pinpoint causes of complaints, and caffeine production and consumption increasing, around 1934, the psychiatry field was officially founded.

Doctors, including psychiatrists, because every psychiatrist is a medical doctor, have had over 100 years to discover causes of mental illness, but stimulated persons commonly lose the ability to properly rationalize, and most everyone ingests caffeine, including doctors and researchers. In other words, the cycle of malfunctioning minds began over 100 years ago, but many people cannot tell that stress and caffeine warped their brain function. How then would people know to condemn stress and caffeine as causes of mental illness?

Trudy Hanley may have told you why mental status changes occur. Unfortunately, the widow collapsed, face down in the street, after leaving Muldoon's Coffeehouse.

3
All The King's Horses

Photo by Allan Kilgour

Paranoid that colleagues would steal his idea, Dr. Langford decided to sponsor a meeting. Looking through the oval office window, Vincent Langford instructed his wife, Eleanor, to send fifty invitations on fine paper. "Mention dinner: roast duck, pumpkin soup, dessert, coffee, or whatever Lucille can prepare to sway a crowd," he said. If thirty doctors attended the event, Langford would be satisfied.

One by one, forty-two doctors knocked at the Langford residence. An oversized Federation, boasting thick porch columns and a great meeting hall, the house was well suited for a grand affair.

Maggie welcomed guests. Dressed in a brown cotton dress cuffed at the wrists and neck, the housekeeper smiled, accepting overcoats.

Reaching for a tobacco stick in a glass jar, on a side table smelling of lime, Dr. Clarke asked, "Dr. Hubert, why are we here?"

Irritated by the young doctor's nonchalant attitude, Dr. Hubert sighed. "To discuss Langford's brilliance."

"And what may that be?"

"Don't you read the medical *Newsletter*?" Hubert tapped a demure waitress on the shoulder, to request another cup of coffee.

Dr. Melrose chimed in, "I read it. Dr. Langford believes a new group of symptoms are psychoneurotic in nature." As Dr. Melrose laughed, doctors turned their heads and stared.

"Dr. Melrose," Hubert stated, overtly, "you shouldn't laugh about the human mind. Haven't you encountered a patient that complains about strange symptoms, symptoms that don't fit a medical picture? For instance: jitters, headache, stomach pain, or restlessness? Just last week, a young lady, pretty little thing, complained about odd sensations, a feeling of bugs crawling along her limbs. Looking around the home, I noted poor lighting, tattered linens and a scraggly cat. Needing attention, the child obviously made up her symptoms."

"Don't be absurd!" Appalled, Dr. Clarke disliked Dr. Hubert insulting his intelligence. "Bleak conditions do not encourage someone to fabricate symptoms."

"Surely, you're amusing us, Dr. Hubert." Dr. Melrose agreed with Clarke. "From the ridiculous does not stem the absurd."

"The others disagree, doctors," Hubert said, sliding a coffee cup from the silver tray. "Oppressive conditions cause people to fantasize about being ill, and until you encounter a case, you'll not know for certain."

"Suppose something patients come across is causing the symptoms, for instance, mortar." Clarke remained firm. "Houses are being constructed. Isn't it possible mortar dust enters the nose and poisons the bloodstream?"

Lifting his cup, Dr. Hubert stressed, "I've heard enough." He walked away from the little group.

Nine blocks away, Trudy Hanley hosted a small gathering in her colonial. Doreen Mulkern offered to open her door to the ladies, but Trudy insisted they gather at her house, "to finish the tapestry samplers for the school and view the scene across the way."

Standing in the doorway, with Kitty close behind, Elise ogled the crowd across the street, outside the coffeehouse. "Doesn't it bother you, Trudy?" Elise asked.

Modest, compared with the others, Maura peered at the stone hearth's blazing fire, spitting in the front room. "Get away from the door, girls. No need to make a spectacle of yourselves."

"Yes. Come along," Trudy said. Hugging her friends, Trudy escorted the ladies to the parlor.

"He had a nerve," Doreen said, "opening a coffee place so close to our houses. And to think, the town approved it."

"The men wanted it." Her face reddening, Kitty yanked a canvas piece from a burlap bag. "And the men are the town."

"Not my Tim." Mabel shook a finger. "The last time he stopped into Muldoon's was the last time. He ran into the house claiming bugs were crawling on his legs. I lifted his trousers and said, 'There's not a thing on your skin but overgrown hair.' He had treated himself to three cups of coffee and a piece of apple pie. 'Must be the pie,' I said joking, 'because the poison wouldn't do it.'"

"'Poison'?" Doreen, with a third grade education, seemed confused.

"I heard that coffee berries grow on plants, like red berries on the bushes along our streets, and the birds won't eat them. 'Tim,' I said, 'if you eat plants, you get bugs.' He didn't find the situation humorous. Complaining about stomach pain, he trotted to bed."

"My oldest would like her husband to take to bed. My Patience wants a baby, but Thurston loves coffee, and he can't. Well, girls, you know what I'm trying to say."

"Enough, Elise." Maura pulled a blue thread through her canvas. "We shouldn't be discussing intimate issues."

"The man up the street became hysterical after drinking coffee at the place. His wife was near paralyzed with fear." Trudy tossed a log onto the fire. "Attacking the wall with a chisel, her husband appeared to drown in his own perspiration. It took three hours for him to come to his senses. The wife wanted to bring a doctor in, but I told her a doctor might claim it was in his head and send him away."

"There's a need to expand the asylum," Dr. Jones stated. "More patients are developing hysteria, and the poorhouses are overcrowded."

"Indeed," Dr. Hubert agreed. "Or perhaps men from the local towns will vote to build another lunatic hospital."

"There's plenty of room on Grange Hill," Dr. Sims said, glancing around, looking for a waitress. "I would like more coffee. How about you, fellows?" Jones and Hubert handed Sims their cups.

Offering peach pie, Trudy said she didn't keep coffee in her home. "Only tea. Does anyone want any?"

Elise held up her glass. "The warm lemonade is fine with me. One cup of coffee in the morning is all anyone needs."

At the other gathering, twelve hands reached for ten cups. Maggie said she would ask Bridget to make more coffee.

After hearing a scream, the friends pulled the curtains and saw the blacksmith's son firing rocks at a horse. Beneath a carriage, dirt smudged on her face and knees, the town seamstress hid, shouting for help. Three arguing loiterers dulled her cries. A man exited the coffeehouse, grabbed the youngster by his neck, and dragged him inside the place. Seconds later, a bearded beanpole of a man pulled the rascal from Muldoon's Coffeehouse and kicked him on his back.

"This has got to stop!" Elise hollered. "First the young man stones the horses, and then the giant beats the rascal!"

Dr. Hubert reached for a plate of cheese. "Dr. Lyons, it's apparent that illness produced by the mind can include a tendency to violence."

Repositioning his legs, Dr. Lyons impatiently waited for dinner. "I agree," he stated, dully. "What is your take, Dr. Belton?"

Passing the small group, en route to the porch, to enjoy a pipe, Dr. Belton halted. "We must help our patients; restrain them at the asylum, prevent them from harming themselves or another."

Maura, Doreen and Mabel slipped on their drab coats. "Aren't you coming along, Elise?" Maura asked, looking forward to walking with her friend.

"I'm going across the street, that's where I'm going," Elise huffed. "To speak with the owner."

Maura warned against it, then Doreen told headstrong Elise to mind her own business. Insisting something had to be done, Elise ignored the women stepping into the misty evening.

Buttoning her hand-stitched coat, Trudy said she'd accompany Elise. "No sense in you entering the place alone."

"I heard Peggy Lawson's husband spent every last penny at Dineen's coffeehouse," Elise said, charging across the street. "The poor man came home, shook his pants, looking for money, but he spent it. Bought every man in the place a cup of coffee and pie, he did."

"Dr. Sims, wouldn't you agree that psychoneurotic illness includes a tendency to spend excessively?" Dr. Hubert reached for a sugar wafer.

"Yes, of course." Sims sniffed a cookie. "The delusions start controlling the wallet, it would seem." The physicians laughed.

"Delusions do not control the wallet," Dr. Clarke croaked, passing the doctors, on his way to the banquet room. "Must I remind you that delusions are assumed to be from abnormal brain function?"

"Rebellious," Hubert quipped. Dr. Sims agreed.

Trudy reminded Elise to keep a level head. "I don't care about the neighbors, mind you, but my son doesn't need to see our names in the *Morning Page*." Holding hands, the women hurried into the coffeehouse.

"Mr. Muldoon," Elise boldly addressed the robust fellow wiping a table. "I think it's time we talk."

A hefty man with a meager mustache, Tristan Muldoon asked what the women needed. Eager to make money, he wanted the ladies to leave.

"Peace of mind," Trudy said, at the counter, eyeing patrons.

Approved for twenty men, the coffeehouse held twenty-eight that evening, cause for a fire. Elise let the owner know.

"No fire here," Muldoon snapped, "except the one from your mouth."

Horsing around with a group of fishermen straight from a profitable catch, a ruddy fellow, looking like he swallowed too much rice pudding, warned, "This isn't a place for women. Go home!"

Raising their cups, four men chanted, "Go home! Go home!"

Sweat and coffee smells sickened Elise. She got to the point: "We're here to discuss the noise, more so the violence. We saw a boy throwing rocks this evening, and several men—"

"Get out!" Jackson Lindquist towered over the ladies. "Leave now!"

As the women raced for the door, three silver spoons flew across the room and hit Trudy on the back. She nervously fled the coffeehouse.

"That didn't get us anywhere!" Elise roared, stepping into the street. Trudy shuffled behind, hoping her nerves calmed down.

Discouraged, the woman didn't know what to do next. Proud of their start, they remained determined to rid the town of the coffeehouse.

"Look out!" Elise watched an object fly. The egg-shaped rock missed Trudy, but the incident harmed her. Trudy collapsed, face down, on the cold ground, breaking her teeth and worse.

"A nail went through her flesh," Tristan Muldoon said, pulling the squarehead out of Trudy's warm chest. "Her heart stopped." He grabbed the widow by the legs and dragged her toward the coffeehouse.

Stroking her friend's face, Elise informed him that Trudy was forty-eight years old. "A respected widow with a son. He's a fine man."

"Your friend's death is sudden, but many things happen when they shouldn't," Muldoon said.

Across town, Dr. Hughes bellowed, "It's apparent that illness produced by the mind includes a tendency to violence and delusions of wealth."

Heading a banquet table, Dr. Sims stressed that doctors must help patients who fabricate physical symptoms.

Dr. Houseman stated, "It is our obligation to restrain patients and prevent them from being a danger to themselves and society."

Outnumbered, sensing defeat, Dr. Melrose and Dr. Clarke reluctantly agreed.

4
Leon's Misfortune

Dedicated to Dave, "Hambone"

On a sultry July afternoon, in 1852, the smell of coffee lingered in Eli's Coffeehouse, a small room in Plainville, a farm and mill town. Lost in the Saturday, six men discussed trivial issues, including how to approach Samuel Simpson and ask him to straighten the fence posts running along his property.

"Such a sight shouldn't be allowed in town," Malcolm Dayton, the town clerk, stated.

Amos Burnell spooned brown sugar into his heavy cup and wholeheartedly agreed. "Furlong cleaned up his yard, and so shall Simpson straighten his crooked fence."

"But he's not well. Massey's death took its toll." Preacher Wagner reached for a glass of rye. "The Lord have mercy on the widower."

Storming into Eli's place, Nick Haglund disrupted the conversation. "Who stole my pigs?" he asked. Deep-set eyes viciously stabbed each man. Accustomed to their father's outbursts, the Morris brothers lifted their cups. Careful not to spill hot brew, they hurried to another table.

"Slow down, Nick," the preacher instructed. "No sense in accusing people without proper evidence."

Nick pounded the table. "I have evidence. Last night I counted twenty-seven pigs. This morning, after my eggs and coffee, I counted twenty-five! Who stole them?"

"No one here took your pigs, Nick." Eli continued, "We're your friends. For God's sake, your cheeks are on fire, and you're all sweaty. Get hold of yourself!" Grabbing Nick's collar, Eli demanded he sit.

Nick fished his pocket for a tobacco pouch. "When I find out who stole my pigs, I'll cut his fingers off!"

"As it should be." Malcolm clapped. "But there hasn't been a theft in town for more than ten months. Drink some coffee and rest your mind."

Relieved to be rid of the lot, Eli wondered about his helper. From the dark side of town, never late, Leon Reed worked from noon until closing on Saturdays.

Focused on rays glittering between towering trees at the trail's end, Leon held tight his rabbit's foot. On the glorious day, he had finished stacking wood for Aunt Pea, his mother's weak sister, from the Bayou. Running, he hoped Eli understood the necessity of his tardiness.

Spotting a lean dog behind a patch of blueberry bushes, Leon panicked. Running faster, he feared the animal attacking. A dog once bit Leon clean to the shinbone. His leg oozed pus for weeks.

Leon could've taken the long path or cut across the field parallel to Nick Haglund's land, but Leon knew last thing the whitey wanted was a colored boy sprinting through tall grass. Afraid for his legs and life, feeling his feet pulse, Leon ran toward high grass. Behind the hysterical teen, the mutt dashed. Leon rubbed his rabbit's foot, praying the dog disappeared and Nick didn't appear.

Rolling tobacco, Nick rubbed his eyes. He believed he was dreaming, hallucinating, seeing an apparition. He took a mouthful of coffee, blinked, then blinked again, willing the sight away, but it remained. "There's a damn blackie in my field!" Nick shouted. "A blackie!" Nick jumped from his side porch.

Sedate in his being, the preacher opened the front gate leading to his quaint four-room home, wondering about Nick. He was crazed like a bat, the preacher thought.

With his adrenaline rising, the farmer convinced himself Leon had stolen his pigs. "You took my pigs! You, boy! You stole my pigs!" Rifle in hand, shouting racial insults, Nick leaped over the log fence.

Nick pointed the gun at the sky. The first shot cracked the silent air. A weak howl erupted before the dog changed direction. It was too late for Leon to turn back. The second bullet hit a weeping willow. Dropping to the ground, Leon released the rabbit's foot.

"What's the ruckus?" Malcolm yelled, carrying an antique axe, its handle splintered. Following Nick, Malcolm sprung over the fence.

"That's the one who stole my pigs!" Nick snitched, unable to keep his thoughts. Again, Nick fired the rifle. "Black thief!"

"Spare me, Lord," Leon prayed out loud. "I swear: I'll never be in this field again." On all fours, he scrambled.

"Perhaps Nick miscalculated," the preacher said to his wife and son. "Something's not right. I'm going over there."

"Get him!" Malcolm shouted, running behind Nick.

"You stole my pigs, boy!" Nick aimed the gun at Leon's head.

Bellying across spiny grass, Leon begged, "Please don't harm me!"

"Get up!" Nick ordered. "Get up and pay the price for theft!"

"I didn't steal nothing! I swear!"

Aware of the men in the field, the man of God counted, "19… 26, 27. You made a mistake, Nick!" The preacher fled. "A mistake!"

Squeezing Leon's stiff ringlets, Malcolm raised the youngster to his feet and dragged the boy to an ant-infested tree trunk. "You should pray they eat you before we crucify you, you black son of a bitch!" Losing bladder control, Leon wet his overalls.

"We'll take two!" Hopping mad, Nick flattened the boy's hand against the trunk.

"A mistake!" the preacher hollered, trying to clear the fence.

Not wanting one drop of Negro blood soiling his shirt, Malcolm handed Nick the axe. "It's your place."

"Please, Lord, no!" Leon writhed in vain.

Forty feet away, his eyes trying to move the quivering axe, the preacher let out a blood-curdling scream. Bathed in sweat, limbs tense as wire, Nick lowered the axe. Slipping, the blade chopped off Leon's right hand.

5
Homeward Bound

Dedicated to Gene and Georgia

As the crowd rushed down the *Brittalica's* plank, a young adult ran by the mob. Six hours early, lugging a heavy sack over his left shoulder, Thomas O'Malley was heading home. The man had hoped to stay in the city, earn a decent wage, and meet a respectable woman, but the town decided his fate after he entered Kelsey's Pub.

During the city's worst thunderstorm of the year, tugging his drenched sweater from his shivering body, Thomas entered Kelsey's Pub, grateful for refuge from the harsh wind. The lantern-lit pub was near empty. Kelsey, June and a stranger huddled at the bar, drinking coffee.

Squeezing his tweed cap over potted ivy, Thomas said hello to Kelsey. The proprietor returned the cordiality, but the outsider stared, wondering why Thomas rung his cap like a sissy. Thomas wandered to a table near the windows, recalling the man in Ireland that eyeballed him.

On a stone pier at Bantry Bay, as young Thomas pedaled by him, a stranger murdered him with his eyes. The following day, the front page of the *Cork Paper* mentioned that Garvey McQuade had waited for his landlord, jumped him from behind, and slashed his throat with a fishhook.

Content sitting alone, Thomas gazed through a fogged window, unaware Kelsey and the stranger left the bar. A smidgen under five feet, June approached.

She looked worried, and Thomas wanted to ask, "Are you feeling all right, June?" He could offer her a warm room for comfort, but couldn't shake the warning he heard after his brother stole a basket of apples.

"Don't yehbe minding no one's business butyeh own!" Anna had screamed. Beating fourteen-year-old Paul with a broomstick, Mrs. O'Malley went wild. "I don't care if the O'Hearn boy talkedyeh into it! Yeh know to keep to yehself!"

The morning the brothers sailed, Anna reminded them to keep to their own affairs. "And keepyeh affairs yeh own."

Thomas ordered pot roast and beer. June smiled, a light smile, not

27

one of glee, recalling her cousin's words. "Get a nice man," Lindy had preached. "The world is too cold for a server trying to make it on her own." She urged June to think about the arrival. "Don't be thinking of anyone else."

Carrying a glass of beer, June sauntered across the pine floor, monitoring her breathing. A new symptom, dizziness came and went. Breathing fast, June reached for a table, hoping to steady herself. Watching the waitress fall, Thomas knew what to do. Grabbing his cap, he stood and raced for the door.

Trudging along slippery cobblestones, Thomas prayed his landlord started a fire in his hearth. Eight rooms, no matter how many logs burned, the boarding house remained damp.

Cursing the mud, the stranger from the pub followed Thomas. "Slow down!" he demanded. "What did you do to her?"

He knew June looked sick, but Thomas hadn't associated with her on the outside, and he certainly didn't know about her dilemma. Conscience clear, Thomas walked faster, noting the carriage stop to let out the bookseller.

Unaware that June had blamed him for her condition, the mild man reached for the wool blanket. Six hours later, greeting dawn, Thomas smiled, noting the stormy skies retreated.

"A sunny one, today," Paul said, slapping Armand the grocer on the back. Unusually tall for his fatness, the store's owner poured Paul a cup of coffee, but never returned the greeting. Deep in thought, Armand recalled the stranger racing by his parlor window, in the rain, shouting at Thomas. He wondered what Thomas had done.

Sitting on stacked grain bags, Thomas dodged coffee odor rising from his brother's cup. He coughed a fake cough.

"Quit the malarkey," Paul ordered. "I know you don't like it, but everyone drinks the brew."

Part of a small crew, the brothers helped layer the hospital's foundation. They loaded stones into a wooden wheelbarrow and rushed them to the site. The men stopped once to eat lunch, once for internal relief, and four times to quench their thirst.

Sipping water, Thomas watched the others. They drank coffee, with one exception. Angus McLeod raised a tarnished flask, defending his inebriation: "To warm me insides."

Thomas studied his brother and Dean, a Canadian immigrant. Pacing the site, Paul and Dean conversed in a serious manner.

As the clock on St. Mary's struck five, Rory MacKenzie tapped Thomas on the back. "I don't like being the one to say this," Rory stated, "but after you abandoned June Fowler, it's best you don't come back. We don't appreciate your kind."

"What are you talking about?" Thomas turned and stared at his brother. "What's this about, Rory?"

"No need for me to slop your business out loud."

Fearing his mother would cane him, Thomas decided against hurling a rock at the milk cart, ambling their way. Politely as he could, given the situation, he asked what Rory expected his brother and him to do. They had been in the city for near eleven months and had saved some, but not enough money to idle.

"Paul stays," Rory said, and lit a slim one. "You go."

Hurrying up the road, Thomas pressed Paul. "What do you know? Tell me what you know! Did someone say something?"

"I heard you left June in a bad way," Paul said, anxiously.

"'A bad way'? You're joking! I don't know the woman!"

"A few men said June fell, and you abandoned her. Not proper for a new father. How about a sweet?" Changing the subject, Paul hoped Thomas would stop discussing the situation. He wanted the problem to go away.

"'A new father'? I'm not anyone's father, Paul! You know that!"

"I'm not with you around the clock," Paul joked, nervously. "Let's get a sweet."

"'A sweet'? How will I pay my board? How will I eat?"

"You should've thought about that before you touched her."

"I haven't put a finger on June! I swear on our father's grave, I never set in public with her." Thomas claimed it was a mix-up. "A terrible mistake."

"If it's a mistake," Paul said, knowing it was, "you better fix it, and fast. Word travels."

Thomas ordered a pack of White Paw Tobacco. He waited, but Armand didn't budge. "Tobacco, Armand."

"I heard you but can't serve you."

Speechless, Thomas left the store. Oblivious to a man reprimanding his toddler son for throwing a pebble at a carriage, he spit on the street.

"Armand, you heard?" Paul handed the grocer a dollar. "Thomas says 'it's a terrible mistake.' Maybe it's a joke."

"No one jokes in this town." Watching Thomas spit, Armand set a pint bottle on the counter. "And no girl fibs about something that serious. It's a sad day when a man refuses to own up to his doings."

Paul asked for White Paw. "To make him feel better."

"Tell him to watch it. Men around here don't take to lying."

Worried, Thomas hustled along Joy Street. "I'll march in Kelsey's and ask why she's lying," he said. "I'll speak to her, Paul."

Knowing the situation had gone too far, Paul panicked. "Don't do that!" *He can't find out.* Paul slapped his brother's arm. "I'll buy you a sweet at Sherman's Coffee House. We'll talk there."

Tying his boots, Thomas looked at his brother, remembering the freckled fellow offering him an apple. Something seemed odd, he knew.

"Look what the cat dragged in!" A painter raised his glass. "The Ireland twins!"

"Stop it, Petrow," Paul ordered, then thought, Someone, help me. He threw his cap at the bearded worker. "You know we aren't twins." *I hope he doesn't know. Does he know?* Paul wiped sweat, trickling from his high forehead.

"He's tamer than you, Paul, but not for long, considering he's to be a father," Petrow said, then laughed. "A toast to the new father!" Snorting, eight workers lifted their hot cups.

"I can't serve you." Mr. Sherman pointed at the door. "Not after what you did. Sorry, Tom."

"Aw, let him stay!" Petrow yelled.

"Rules are rules, Petrow. You keep shut!"

Paul ordered his brother to wait outside. "I'll purchase the whole cherry pie for you," he said, in his delusional state, believing the treat would miraculously cure the problem.

"Liar!" a man shouted, passing Thomas on the dirt sidewalk.

Hollow-eyed, a stranger spit at Thomas. Paul grabbed his brother as he lunged at the man. "He's a sinner!" the man yelled, scurrying up the road.

Thomas leaned against the brick coffeehouse, eating the last bite of pie. Then he swallowed hard, said goodbye to his brother, and fled.

The landlord refused to let him in. "I was having tea with Mrs. Rutherford, downstairs, when I heard about the trouble you caused." Mrs. Burns shook a newspaper. "You refuse to own up to it? We'll see about that!" Slamming the door, she said Thomas wasn't welcome there.

"What about my belongings? My clothes and the picture of my mother? Please, let me in!"

"Send your brother!"

Thomas marched twelve blocks, hiked the steps, and knocked on the chipped brown triple-decker. "Your brother's not there," an elderly man, drinking tea on the porch next door, offered. "He left a little while ago, to find someone." Tipping his cap, Thomas thanked the curiosity seeker. The old man ordered him to stay out of the neighborhood.

"Take your money, Dean." Behind St. Mary's church, Paul shoved a handful of dollars at the mason. "My brother's in trouble. Take it."

"We had an agreement," Dean said, pushing Paul. "I'm warning you. There'll be trouble if you break the deal!"

"The baby's yours," Paul reminded Dean. "June's baby is not my brother's!"

"I'll slice your throat to the cords if you talk!"

"But Thomas is innocent!" Paul persisted, "He can't live like this, without a job, thrown out of every shop in town!" *How did I get into this mess! My brother!*

"You should have thought of that before you stuck your hand out!"

I never thought about the consequences! "But I didn't think this would happen!" *I thought about the money! Something went wrong in my head! What's wrong with me?* "Please," Paul begged. "Take the money!"

Dean hurried toward the path in the woods. Looking back, he warned, "Don't mess with me again! I paid you to keep your trap shut!"

The high moon nearly wept as Paul carried his brother's belongings to the street. Ashamed of himself, wondering why he sold his blood's good name, Paul stacked a heavy sack and blanket on an empty onion box, then he reached into his pocket and grabbed a ticket. "I'm sending you home. Get on the ship and don't look back! There's nothing here for you, for us. I'll be home in the spring."

Jogging to the dock, eagerly looking forward to departing the land of the living dead, Thomas wondered why people didn't give him the opportunity to defend himself. Knowing society had wronged him, he questioned what changed stability of reasoning.

Crazed from his faulty chemistry, Paul obsessed about selling his brother out. What possessed me to do it? he repeatedly asked himself, rushing to the corner coffeehouse.

6
In The Web

Photographer, Mike Dijital

Hours of writing with the aid of poor lighting and pools of black coffee exhausted Edward Leary. Painful, his hands had cracked from lack of fats and water. His limbs ached, and a dull throb burned the back of his neck. Almost overnight, fine lines appeared in Edward's face.

Past the breaking point, refusing to doze, Edward sat at his desk, staring at the open window and large sparrow perched on the sill. "It can't be," Edward uttered, rubbing his eyes. "Surely, the thing's not real." Jumping from his chair to investigate, Edward knocked over his tin coffee cup. Tepid fluid ran onto the writing tablet and splashed his wrinkled shirt. Wiping the puddle with a hand, Edward dragged coffee across the desk.

Believing if he remained quiet the bird would stay put, Edward tiptoed toward the sill. Beady eyes, visible only to Edward, returned Edward's stare.

Arm's length away, Edward believed he poked starchy, gray feathers. "It's real!" Face ashen, legs and hands trembling, Edward darted to the kitchen. He settled for the dregs.

"It's not as though he's hurting me." Edward pushed a rag across the wet items. "He is distracting me."

Ignoring the hallucination, a fountain pen in hand, Edward dully stated, "Write as if someone is pushing you out to sea, and you yearn to bob in clear waters," his father's words. "Write with every ounce of courage, every bit of stamina and your heart and soul buried in the pages. Write, my son. Find a subject one has not conjured and one day, the spirits willing, you will achieve great success. And maybe not." Edward dropped his pen and lifted the coffee cup.

A sweet string of words danced in the air: "You know you want to fly. Fly with me, Edward."

Edward told himself to get some sleep, "because that bird can't be real. It's not possible." And yet, he sat, suspended between two worlds, not knowing he was demented.

Edward's wife asked if he heard her. On her way to bed, Abigail had pled with him to accompany her.

"Look at the bird!" Edward reached for the feathered fellow. "His size is extraordinary!" A flash of twinkling lights shot across Edward's eyes, and the imaginary bird vanished.

Edward looked at the bookcase and then the floor. "You must believe me! Clear as day, I swear! A good four feet he is, with prickly feathers and a melodic voice. Ha!" Edward's tongue flickered from its dark cavern, licking parched lips.

Abby lowered her head. "A bird spoke?"

"Yes, and his enunciation is quite good, if I do say." A mad laugh escaped Edward as he alligatored across the floor.

Afraid to caress Edward's moist forehead, the good wife begged, "Come to bed. You need sleep."

"My hours are ten each day." Edward grabbed a comer of the desk, pulling himself to his feet. "Ten each day!" He reached for the stained coffee cup.

Abby flitted across the pitted wood floor. "It's not real," she warned. "It's in your mind."

Edward's voice trailed: "It is real!"

"And last week it was Michael." A finger rattled the air. "Angels appear for the dying and dead. "And you're not dead."

Twenty-nine years old, Edward was closer to the grave than they knew. Since his youth, with each taste of caffeine, his brain tinkered with madness. The legal psychoactive drug had finally swept him into the vortex of lost souls.

From the bedroom, Abigail threatened to call Dr. Rooslet. Deeply fogged, Edward ignored her.

The Press had published two short stories, *The Rooster and the Mare* and *Samuel's Bride*. The pay barely kept the four-room, third-floor flat, but Edward refused to ask his father for additional help. An elderly gent, fifty-two years old, a senior accountant with the First Nation Bank, Sean Leary flaunted his embarrassment of his son each time he assisted Edward financially. "Do something with your life," Sean had ordered, the last time he opened his billfold for his son. "Get a decent job."

Edward's mind jitterbugged, rapidly turning thoughts over: *A tailor, a doctor, a nurse, a constable, a doctor, dead, deadly, alive...* He needed an idea, a subject a writer hadn't touched upon, to satisfy readers and purchase the house on Ludlow Street, the ten-roomer Abby admired. Tweaking a corner of his beard, the writer let go a foreign squeak. "Suicide from ether. Ha, ha!" Edward decided to speak with Dr. Rooslet.

Making it a point to speak with Edward, Dr. Rooslet trotted across Main Street. Abigail's knocking on his door before breakfast concerned him. Surely, he thought, the man hasn't gone mad. He knew Sean Leary's son could accomplish much.

Sipping coffee, Edward thought about the new day and a need to write. *Write like the wind,* his father's voice in his head ordered. *Write your way to fame or put down the pen.*

"Edward," the bird sung, sugary. "Fly with me."

"Shoo, shoo, out!" Edward screamed, haunted by the past and the bird. Negative memories and the hallucination persisted.

"Don't deprive yourself. Remember you wanted to soar like the ducks on your eighth Christmas?" the bird asked. "Your father said, 'No, my son. People can't fly. Step away from the pond.' He was wrong. People fly all the time, their arms flapping with the wind."

Edward's mind drifted: *People can't fly. Step away from the pond and we'll shoot a duck or two. Then you'll be a fine hunter.*

"Trust me, Edward. Think what you can write after your trip. Your father will be proud of you."

Swallowing coffee, Edward considered flying. The more he ingested, the more the idea made sense. "I can fly over town and recall all I see, jot memories and share the public." Edward reached for the cup. "Yes, yes, my father will be proud!"

One foot swung over the ledge. "That's it," the sparrow urged. "Hold my hand."

The hallucination encouraged Edward to ignore the door. "It's not important. You're the most important person, Edward. People will envy you for flying," the sparrow insisted.

Avoiding Dr. Rooslet hollering in the hall, Edward gripped the sill. With one foot dangling outside the apartment, the other leg in, he looked down. On the street, a ragman spoke with factory workers, mothers held little hands, dogs surrounded Russo's Meat Market and a worker steadied a ladder against a streetlamp. The street hummed, but in Edward's mind everything moved slowly.

"I'm coming in!" With one kick, the doctor broke the door.

"Flap your arms!" the bird ordered.

Witnessing Edward preparing to plunge onto the street, Dr. Rooslet pleaded with him to reconsider. Up and down, Edward's lips moved, but he never emitted a sound.

The doctor grabbed Edward's shirt tale and pulled him to the floor. He demanded to know what Edward had seen.

Drenched in perspiration, his heart beating madly, Edward pointed to the sill. "The sparrow," he said, but Edward's hallucination had disappeared, and according to Dr. Rooslet, Edward had vanished, too.

Helping Edward with his coat, the doctor explained that he was taking him across town, to his office. Craving adrenaline, Edward asked for a cup of coffee. The doctor assured him there would be coffee at the office.

Above Mendel's Warehouse, Dr. Rooslet unlocked the door to his private asylum. The less fortunate stayed at the state hospital, but the privileged avoided it. Dr. Rooslet knew the senior Leary would pay to keep his son's condition away from the public.

Dr. Rooslet began, "Do you have problems with your mother?"

Why does he ask about my mother? "No." Squirming on a hard chair, Edward picked his hands.

The doctor asked why he scratched his flesh.

"It's as though bugs are all over me."

"I see. Would you like more coffee?"

"Please," Edward said, dropping the striped cup. It hit the floor, cracking in fourteen places. "I'm sorry, I'm sorry." *And now the duck is on the ground, son, but you spoiled it, shooting it in the wrong place.*

In the morning, feeling Edward's forehead, Dr. Rooslet remarked, "You're burning up, son. Feverish, excited, nervous, confused, delusions. This is not good, Edward. It all points to dementia praecox."

"No, can't be. Must be a mix-up. No craziness in my family. No, no, that's all wrong. I'm a writer. Just tired. Need to go home." *Back to the house. There's always next year.* Cackling, Edward stood. "Next year, I'll be back. Got to shoot a duck in the right place. Don't get the wrong spot, ho, ho, you fool!"

"Edward, did you hear what I said? You have dementia praecox." Handing a nurse a key, Dr. Rooslet ordered Phyllis to prepare room 4. "No one but your family will know."

"'Dementia praecox'?" Abigail asked and frowned. "How is that ever possible?"

"Dementia praecox is a fairly new disorder. It comes on suddenly and affects approximately one person in 4,000."

Two determined nurses pushed Edward into an ice bath. The water burned his flesh. *You must learn to swim, son. And he shoved me under— under—under!* "Help! Up! Get me up!" Edward pushed against four arms.

Phyllis toweled goosebumped flesh. "You'll sleep well, Mr. Leary."

Locking Edward's door, Phyllis asked God to take the young man. "Bring him peace," she said, making the sign of the cross in the air. Then she strolled to room 3.

Dr. Rooslet handed Sean Leary a cup of coffee and said, "For sixty-two dollars a month, I'll keep him here, at my hospital, if that's agreeable."

"My good doctor, I've known something is different. He's not like my other two children. Sean followed in my footsteps. He has a promising position at the bank. But that one? He wanted to be a writer. Evidently, his imagination arises from insanity. 'No cure,' you say, and I believe you. You know where to send the bills."

"Good afternoon, Edward. Today is 489 of your stay, and you don't seem to be improving. It's time we try hypnosis," Dr. Rooslet said, patting a pillow. "Do you want anything before we start?"

"I'd like bl-bl-black coffee."

The physician opened the door. "Phyllis, bring a cup of coffee for Edward!"

7
Simon

Dedicated to Jim

Leaning against glass doors, separating the parlor from the dining room, Simon feared the inevitable. Death. With the walls seeming as if they closed in on him, he wanted to flee the family home. Coping with nasal rhinitis, Simon coughed hard, trembled and had lost weight. "I'm going for a walk," he said, anxious to move his rigid legs.

"You shouldn't," Darlene cautioned. Leading her brother to a highback chair near the wood stove, she urged him to relax. "You must stop trembling," she said. "It's not good when the body shakes." Offering to bring Simon tea, Darlene patted little Jeffrey on the head, slipped by Sarah's girls playing marbles on the floor, and hustled to the kitchen.

Sarah poured tea. "I don't know what's become of Simon," she said. "The doctor said Parkinson's disease is a lifetime illness, but he's too young for an old man's disease. The doctor said he would be fine. He said we should give it time, but he seems ill."

"He'll have to stay another week," Darlene stated. "We'll bring him back to health."

"Do you have anything for us, Uncle Simon?" Tompkins tugged his uncle's hand. Sweaty, it greeted the boy weakly. "Do you?"

"I don't have any candy tonight, little ones," Simon said, discouraged.

"Please, Simon, you've got to have a sweet," blonde, blue-eyed Laura, second youngest of the bunch, pleaded. Simon coughed.

The harsh sound had rattled Simon's insides for more than a week. The doctor assured him he'd be better in a few days, but Simon was getting worse. He worried about being near the children, but his sisters forbid him to return to his place until he recovered.

Not one relative showed signs of Simon's illness. Simon suffered alone. Weakness, fever, headaches and white patches on his tongue, obvious symptoms of drug overdose, plagued him.

Simon reached into his pockets, seeking a handkerchief. Quite unusual, his pockets did not carry butterscotch or peppermints for the children. "Anyone for a butterscotch chip?" he asked.

Giddy, Lilabeth jumped on the sofa. "Me! Me!"

Laura tossed an embroidered pillow at Chamberlain. "Uncle Simon's going to bring us something!"

"John's must be open still. I'll go over and see what I can buy."

"Not tonight, children," Darlene said. Handing Simon a warm cup, Darlene mentioned their uncle not feeling well. She offered to stir a batch of fudge and pop corn after they settled down. All nine children listened intently, though not all accepted the words.

"I'll be fine," Simon said. His nose dripped. "I'm restless and could use a walk. The fresh air might do me good."

"There's always tomorrow," Sarah said. "Tonight, I'll read from *Alice in Wonderland* and *Little Black Sambo*. We'll pop corn and eat fudge."

"Butterscotch," Simon said, exciting the children.

Eight-year-old April clapped. Sprawled next to her sister on the floor, twelve-year-old Hope, peacemaker of the group, quietly said, "Uncle Simon is ill. We can pop corn."

"Butterscotch," Simon repeated. Perspiring, his legs wobbly, he strolled to the dining room to fetch his coat.

"You don't look good, Simon." John Landry wrapped hard candies in paper. "Maybe a taste of chocolate will cure whatever ails you." John handed Simon a chocolate almond square, a token of friendship.

With a bite of chocolate left, Simon knew the rattling had increased. Feverish, spitting thin fluid, he hurried back, toward 79 Upland Street.

"Where've you been?" Percy Dalloway hollered, entering his gallant, brick home, as Simon turned the corner of Terrace and Upland. "It's been a long time." Percy waved Simon to the front stairs. "Come in! Come in! Elizabeth will make coffee."

Simon wanted to return to the family home, hand his nieces and nephews candy, watch them smile, and crawl into bed as quickly as possible, but he knew a chat with Percy wouldn't last but a mere half hour. An attorney for Dalloway & Trinket, Percy followed an early to bed, early to rise routine.

"You're coughing, Simon," Elizabeth noted. "Have you the flu?"

"Don't be impolite, honey," Percy said, offering Simon a cigarette. "There's not been any flu in nearly a year. Simon has the Parkinson's."

"I know, but Simon doesn't sound well." Elizabeth placed a blue cup and saucer in front of Simon. "Drink," she said. "Maybe the coffee will heal your insides."

Allergic to caffeine but not knowing, Simon slurped coffee, hoping to finish it before the sun went down. His head ached, and he felt the fluid build in his chest.

"Thank you, Elizabeth," Simon said, at the front door. "It's been a pleasure knowing you both."

"Why so glum?" Percy asked. "We'll see you soon."

I'm not myself. I feel like I'm dying. A bad case of nerves, that's all. Simon rubbed his chest. Perspiring heavily, the worried man traipsed faster, obsessing about his health. *You're ill and you know it. Stop the nonsense! You're daft. I'll be fine after sleep. I'll be fine. The doctor promised I'll be feeling like my old self soon.*

All nine children greeted Simon at the front door. Preoccupied with his unordinary physical state, the kind man handed each child a treat.

Dividing his time, Simon had favored each little person equally. It seemed only right that all nine children stood in the parlor, surrounding the coffin. Unable to control their tears, the children distressed about their loss.

Pulmonary edema murdered twenty-eight-year-old Simon in his sleep, from ongoing allergic response to caffeine—a condition rarely diagnosed by doctors that causes progressive physical and mental decline. Fluid filled Simon's head and lungs. Six-year-old Milton found his uncle in bed. Rigor mortis had set in.

8
Strike Three

Danvers State Hospital
Photo by Jason Baker

"Pull it all!" The young man in a loose-fitting brown suit sprinted by the players jogging from the field. "Take it all while you can!"

"Who's that?" Reggie Dunlap asked. He spit tobacco juice on the ground.

Albert Masey spat, too. "Just another oddball," he replied.

The date: September 29, 1929. The bottom of the fifth. One man on.

"The public should know it's going to fall! It'll drop like a rock from the sky!" On the pitcher's mound, the stranger flagged his arms. "Save your money! Your houses!" As the man shouted a final warning, four men in blue rushed him from behind.

"Master Vickery," Judge Therold stated, "you trespassed, held up a baseball game and disturbed the American people. What do you have to say about your actions?"

Marching in place, David Vickery claimed he was doing his job. He said his father, Senator Stanley Vickery, mentioned the stock market would crash and people should be warned.

"I do not care about your father. It is not your responsibility to preach, unless you're an orator." Raising his voice, the Harvard graduate asked, "Are you a public speaker?"

"No sir. Sir, no, I'm not. No sir." Running his fingers across his slicked-back crew cut, the twenty-two-year-old began crying.

Turning to Attorney Fields, the judge asked if there was a history of mental illness in the Vickery family. Fields was not aware of any mental instability in the Vickery family.

"There is a history of disturbing the peace." Judge Therold flipped through a ledger. "Singing on the streets after midnight, throwing snowballs at automobiles. The list continues. I recommend observation.

40

Thirty days at The Idiot Hospital."

"But, Your Honor, Senator Vickery is out of the country."

"Well, Attorney Fields, we know that his son will be in the country. He is of age. Thirty days."

"The castle?" His eyes widening, Attorney Fields gasped. "But, Your Honor, I'm sure there's another facility, something more conducive to this young man's mental state. Master Vickery is not insane."

"Attorney Fields, the finest physicians are at the hospital on the mount. Would you like to go with him, and bring back a report?"

Anxious to leave the room and dissociate his name with the asylum on the hill, Attorney Fields quietly responded, "I understand, Your Honor. Young Vickery will be well cared for."

A senior nurse escorted David to a yellow room. "This is where you'll spend most of your time," Donna said, grabbing the magazine Marvin hit himself with. "You smell, Marvin. You need a bath." Coiling, Marvin hunched his back. "Not this minute, you old bat." Donna laughed. "He's a regular. Regularly stays and never leaves. Isn't that right, Marvin? No one comes and you just stay. How many years now? Put your fingers up. Your fingers, Marvin, because they can get broken." Twice, Marvin raised ten fingers. "Kathy, get Marvin some chocolate. He's been a good boy." Grinning, Kathy sauntered toward the cubbyhole kitchen.

"Ignore the twins." Spreading her hands to distance the arguing teens, Donna scooted between Peter and Patrick. "Keep it up and you'll be in confinement. They swallowed a batch of paint. Went to their heads. Their parents bring them in when they can't take it any longer."

Blowing saliva bubbles, Leroy stuck a leg out to trip anyone who came close. "Be good, Leroy," Donna ordered, "or I'll hide your teeth."

As David and the nurse walked the hall, David screamed inside his head: *I won't survive here! I don't belong here! Dad, come get me!*

Dismal, the corridor hosted twenty-five doors. Many of the rooms hid men and their illness, one condition, untreated physical illness.

"Tick, tick, tick!" Hammond spurted, madly typing his next novel on an imaginary typewriter. "Tick, tick, tick!"

"Enough, Hammond!" Donna yelled, startling David. Mesmerized by a patient pacing the floor, he stared. "That's Percy," Donna said. "He's harmless."

Back and forth, Percy Talbot walked the hall. Gray at the temples, Percy abruptly halted and saluted a soldier in a dusty green uniform, with three silver buttons on the lapel. The vision stood in a corner, smoking.

"It smells in there, again," Donna complained, unlocking a door.

Naked, in a compact private hell, his stomach drooped to the groin, Ned Foster, retired postman, entertained himself. Sprawled on the floor, the dehydrated man rubbed feces on the wall.

Turning the key, Donna pulled the door shut. "I can't be bothered, because some things never change. Someone else can clean up the mess."

Praying to survive the horrors, David focused on the room. Covered with a sheet and blanket, the bed lacked character. Bars partially hid two windows. A three-drawer chest served as a holding port for personal belongings. Though exceptionally distraught, David appeared composed.

"The bathroom's down the hall," Donna said, indifferently, "and there's a bucket, just in case, beside your bed."

Holding a tin cup, Donna told David that when the door was locked if an emergency arose he should bang the cup on the door. "And not your I'm tired, lonely, or afraid emergencies, because we know you're all that and more."

Irritated, David asked, "What am I supposed to do all day?"

"Talk with Dr. Ronald Newcomb, the psychiatrist. You'll also mingle, eat, sleep, and think. Any more questions?" Hands on her hips, Donna scrunched the standard uniform, hiking it over her knees.

David inquired about coffee. Craving caffeine, he wanted a cup.

Donna chuckled. "This isn't a prison. It's a place for us to help you get well. Everyone here drinks coffee, and most people smoke. They're small pleasures patients look forward to. There's a running percolator here, and someone usually brings pastries, jelly donuts, chocolate macaroons, sugar cookies, something sweet. They go quickly, so you may ask one of us to pick up something at the store. If we can, we usually will, if you're behaving well. If not, you're out of luck. Oh, and ask Kathy or whoever's around to pour your coffee. Last week, old man Carson, you'll meet him, spilt coffee all over himself, then peed on the spot. Kathy wasn't happy."

Leaning against the wall, David slouched on the cot, sipping coffee. Panicky, he tried calming himself, envisioning sliding red checker pieces across a table board, in front of the brick fireplace, next to his father. His skin pallor, temperature rising and chronic cough intensifying, David did not feel well. The chocolate pudding served at dinner had increased his symptoms. "Come get me! Please, Dad, Daphne!" David yelled. "Take me home! Get me out of here! I don't feel good!"

"You want company?" Frankie's slippers crackled, shuffling across the floor. "Shhh," the fat man warned. "Candy wrappers. Have to hide 'em. You got candy?"

David did not have candy, a book, or anything else to occupy his mind. Laden with a thirty-day sentence, he coped with flu-like symptoms.

Dr. Newcomb flipped pages. "Can you tell me why you're here?"

"They said I caused a ruckus," David explained, shifting his legs. He glanced through dirty windows.

"It says here you 'cried in court.'" Coldly, Newcomb eyed the horrified young man.

"Yes, but I was very tired and not feeling well." Tapping his feet on the floor, David said he still felt lousy.

"I see. Well, your pulse is high and white count elevated. Do you have any physical problems?"

"Just a rundown feeling and a cough."

Pulling a Pall Mall from a top pocket, Dr. Newcomb asked about David's episode. "At the ballpark. Do you remember it?"

"Yes, I remember." David sighed. "I wanted to warn people the stock market is going to fall."

Smug in his Captain's chair, Newcomb let go a loud, sinister laugh. "That's a delusion if I ever heard one. But," he continued, reaching for a matchbook, "it all seems to fit. Manic-depression. The up and then the low. Racing pulse, high white count and delusions. I'll speak with Dr. Granby, and I'll see you again in a few days." Newcomb lit the cigarette.

"That isn't possible, sir." David stood. "There's no mental illness in my family. I don't feel well, but no doctor can tell me what's wrong."

Newcomb exhaled smoke. "I just did, Mr. Vickery."

Fleeing, David bumped his chair. "I don't feel well!" he repeated. "I don't feel well!"

Dr. Newcomb documented: "Manic-depression, probably early stage, and hyperchondriasis. Patient claims he doesn't feel well."

"Sure, I did the entrance exam on the Vickery boy," Dr. Granby stated. "He's like the rest of them, complaining he doesn't feel well. Obviously, his symptoms are in his head." Pouring a cup of coffee, Dr. Granby continued, "The boy has a high white count, high pulse, a sense of ill feeling. It all points to manic-depression, Dr. Newcomb. I have faith you'll treat him fine. By the way, I'm leaving for the west coast, day after tomorrow. Dr. Raynard, from across town, will cover."

"I'm sorry," Agatha said, straightening her white cap, "but you can't go in there. The rules are the same for everyone—No visitors or calls for two weeks."

Daphne flung her leather purse onto the desk. "My brother is here, and our father called and told me to take him home."

"You'll have to come back in twelve days." Agatha handed Daphne a hankie. "Cry yourself a river. Twelve days."

Scraping her heels, Daphne laughed. "We'll see who cries."

Scanning a Farmers' Almanac, David sat in the lounge. Every so often he looked at Leroy. Weeping in a corner, Leroy dug his arms. Next to him, on the floor, Gary howled, scratching Leroy's neck.

"Mary, Mother of God!" Kathy shouted, grabbing Leroy's bloody arms. "Someone call a doctor!" Turning, she stared at David. "Why didn't you say something? Are you that deficient you couldn't say something?"

"Calm down!" Donna yelled, running to the scene. "He's the Senator's son!"

"I don't give a damn who he is! He just sat there while this was happening!"

Not my business! David raced to his room. *I'm not an orator!*

"If you don't eat the chicken, I'll shove it down your throat," Nurse Beverly threatened, hovering over David.

Saying David had a bad day, a young nurse intervened. "He's not hungry," she asserted. "Leave him alone. He doesn't feel well."

"Grandiose behavior," Donna documented, looking at David, staring out the window. "Patient prefers his room to mingling. Thinks he's better than the other patients."

After gulping a six-inch chocolate bar Frankie had given him, David recited an *Our Father* and crawled under the blanket. His right leg kicked, then his left.

Focused on his knees moving beneath the blanket, David spotted a nine-inch snake slithering across the wool. He jumped from bed, ran to the door, and jiggled the handle. "Help me! Someone, help me! A giant snake's in here!"

"Hello, young man," Dr. Raynard said, offering his hand. "It says here, you had quite the night. Saw a snake and spiked a temp. Aspirin and ice water brought your temperature down. Is that right?"

"Yes, sir. That's what happened."

Fingering a wrist, Dr. Raynard informed David his pulse was high and asked him to remove his shirt. As David removed the cotton pajama top, the doctor asked what he consumed the day before.

"A chocolate cookie, a piece of toast, a half bowl of beef stew, a few crackers, eight cups of coffee, and some chocolate."

Spotting the rash on David's neck, Dr. Raynard asked how long it had been there. It resembled heat rash.

"A couple of months. I pointed it out to several doctors when I complained about fatigue. They gave me pep pills."

"Caffeine tablets?"

"Yes, sir."

Examining the raised scarlet patch, Dr. Raynard asked if David used drugs. David shook his head.

Knowing something affected David, Dr. Raynard asked what Dr. Granby, in the infirmary, concluded about the rash. In between sobs, David blurted out Granby's assumption, that David irritated himself shaving. David went on to tell the doctor he didn't feel well, no one believed him, and he was getting worse. He grabbed his pajama top and wiped his eyes. Dr. Raynard assured David he would be okay.

Nearing the door, the doctor looked back. David nibbled a chocolate cookie. Dr. Raynard reminded himself to look up drug allergies.

"How come my sister isn't here?" David asked. "My father's away, but Daphne should be here."

Twisting a pencil, Dr. Newcomb claimed not one person inquired about David. "It's for the better," he said. "We need time to treat you."

"I'm not mentally ill." Insistent, David repeated his statement. Stretching his arms over his head, he added, "Maybe some doctors are crazy, and patients are normal. Did you ever think of that?"

"Defiant," Dr. Newcomb scribbled. "You're not funny, young man. Sarcasm is a sign of mental illness. There is no doubt. You are afflicted with manic-depression."

Another restless evening shadowed young Vickery. Trying to avoid the twins arguing about who their mother favored, ignoring Frankie begging for candy, and steering his eyes from Leroy picking himself, David asked Kathy for coffee.

Pacing the hall behind Percy, David heard "Tick, tick, tick!" He laughed, disheartened.

Disturbed by the marchers, Nurse Marjorie sucked her Lucky Strike. Exhaling smoke, Marjorie chirped, "Get to bed, now, you two! Hurry!" Percy and David scattered.

No pets, no books, no phone calls! "Damn it!" David hurled the tin cup at the door. "Damn all of you! Get me out of here!"

"Get Callie!" Kathy ran to David's room. "We have to restrain him! He's in a manic state!"

As three nurses held David, Callie, a hefty, bald orderly, forced

David's arms into a straight jacket. Struggling, David lost the battle.

Locked in the idiot suit, David stared at the wall, swearing at God. For four hours, he hollered. The nurses ignored him.

"Good morning, girls," Dr. Raynard said, glancing at five nurses. "I'll take the Vickery boy his breakfast. No coffee or tea for him." He watched Donna roll her eyes. "You don't have to approve of my doctoring. After all, I'm not here very often, but I am in charge of Master Vickery, and I don't approve of him taking caffeine."

"I'm sorry that happened," Dr. Raynard said, relieving David of the idiot suit. "However, I have good news. I believe you are allergic to caffeine. That explains the fever, lousy feeling, sniffles, racing pulse and abnormal mental changes. You must avoid all products containing caffeine. Perhaps difficult, but you can do it."

For forty-eight hours, feeling like a truck hit him, David drank water. Sleeping, he perspired, soaking the sheets. Diarrhea, anxiety, appetite loss and more entered the withdrawal phase.

With one push, a tall man sporting a navy blue suit and dark derby opened the door. Behind him, a young woman fashioning an aqua dress, with square pearl buttons on the cuffs, followed.

Senator Vickery approached Agatha. "Where is my son?" he asked, pounding the desk.

"Sir," Agatha boldly stated, speaking to the man but staring at Daphne, "we don't do things like that here."

"I don't give a rat's ass what you do here, but I'll tell you what I'll do if my son is not released. I will haul every one of you bastards into Superior Court for kidnapping, not contacting a family member, and other significant poor treatments!" The Senator resembled a McIntosh, ripe from a branch. "I suggest that if you want to keep your job, you go get my son!"

"What do you mean 'allergic to caffeine'?" Searching for a pencil, Dr. Newcomb lifted a stack of papers.

"Exactly what I said." Dr. Raynard dropped a folder on Newcomb's desk. "David Vickery is physically ill, and you and everyone else in here should know that. Look at the symptoms! You all goofed! After he ingests caffeine—his mood exaggerates due to the allergic response. Then, when caffeine is removed from his diet—he goes into a slump, a withdrawal state mistaken for depression."

"Calm down, Dr. Raynard. If your diagnosis is accurate, we can, we can." Dr. Newcomb paused to search his vocabulary bank for words exempting liability. "We shall say that along with his manic-depression a reputable doctor discovered David suffers hypersensitivity to caffeine, rare but possible."

"Excuse me, doctors," Agatha said, interrupting the discussion. "Mr. Vickery insists on speaking with his son's physicians."

Senator Vickery stormed into the room. "Damn you, doctors! My son—and go get him," the Senator ordered, addressing Agatha— "sought care from doctor after doctor, and not one doctor helped him! Not one!"

"The good news is that your son is sick, Senator," Dr. Raynard said.

Senator Vickery hollered, "Of course, he's sick! No wonder he ended up here! Doctors don't know what they're doing! How many other patients are sick? Or don't any of you know?" Offended, Agatha hurried from the room.

"Cry yourself a river," Daphne said, as Agatha skirted around her. "And get a lawyer, a good one."

"Mr. Vickery, your son made a wild assumption that the stock market would fall," Dr. Newcomb said. "Why would he assume such nonsense?"

"Because I told him!" The Senator thumped his chest. "Me, his father, a man who follows the market!"

Newcomb pulled a pencil from behind his left ear. "Here it is," he said, and nervously laughed.

"We cannot do a damn thing about this, Stanley." Attorney Fields offered a Cuban cigar. "Too many people use caffeine, too many doctors are undereducated, and just because the dangers of caffeine are written in books doesn't mean all people read. They don't. Men play cards, play golf, and play women. If you want my advice, take the money the director offered and get on with your life. David's excelling at college, and that's what you should concentrate on. Be happy."

On Tuesday, October 29, 1929, the stock market plunged. After learning of the fall, Ronald Newcomb, M.D. stood on the fourth-floor balcony of the Waltzer Hotel, inhaled deeply, closed his eyes and jumped.

9

Ruben's Journal

Photo by Stewart Whitmore

Entry 52

A lawyer defending clients who try not to shift their eyes toward the floor, I'm proud of my career. Hired last in the firm, I was happy to grab a coffee and slice of lemon pie with the boys, at Sparky's, a deli on the corner of Leverton and West. I never understood what the practice was about, until it was too late.

She was a pretty girl. High cheekbones framed her tight face. Long lashes magnified her eyes. Brown. Big brown eyes, like acorns on a fall day dropped from the spreading oak in my front yard, seemed to cling to me when I suggested. You know.

It rained. Not a spit, fall rain, a heavy downpour, the kind that soaks through every inch of your clothing, freezing you to the bone.

"Five dollars," I offered, cracking the window. Those eyes looked at me as if I'd offered a million. She must've been happy to get out of the rain. "And a bag of chocolate." I winked.

As she climbed into my show car, the red dress hiked to her hips, exposing long, curvy legs. Not one line invaded her face. I guessed she was nineteen, not more than that.

"Your place or mine?" she asked, pulling her black sweater closer to her perfect body. I offered my hand, but the girl refused it. In a "This is strictly business" attitude, she turned to glare out the window. "What will it be? Yours or mine?"

I dug my nails into the steering wheel. My place was definitely not an option. Dee and our three little ones, well, my wife would probably be reading the news and they'd be crawling into bed. Blondie, the retriever, would snuggle next to Dee, his tail jutting out from under the afghan that Dee's mother made, a gift for, maybe a birthday, or no, our fourth anniversary. Blondie sort of took over when I wasn't around, and back then, that was almost every night.

Busy with the partners, I almost forgot I had a family. And with the girl sitting next to me, you'd think I forgot my wife.

It was business, you know, to tell the guys so I could feel like a real comrade. To fit in. I did it to fit in.

"I had a hot one last night, Ruben. It's your turn now," Harry said. "Then tell us." He wagged his tongue perversely, and I laughed. Hell, the man paid me.

It was a game. They all played it. Just a game.

With neighbors peering from their windows, I never considered going through my area. My baby is a difficult car to forget.

"Let me see those beautiful eyes," I said. I wanted her attention. I needed it. I paid for it.

It was only a glance. Her eyes never greeted mine. They focused on my wrist. "A fishing injury," I muttered. "The boys and I go to Maine every year. Sometimes twice." I wouldn't tell her I sliced it. That I slashed a carving knife into my flesh, hoping I'd lose every drop. She would have thought I was a nut case.

Dr. Jacobs called me psychotic, but my mother knew I was okay. "A little melancholy. That's all," my mother said, in the hospital, petting my adolescent, pimpled face.

Through steamed up glass, the girl glared at the receding rain. It let up by the time I pulled the car into the Five & Dime's lot. They serve coffee at the fountain, and I needed a cup.

Handing me two cups of black to go, the fountain clerk told me to have a special night. I didn't know how special it would be.

Funny, I thought, with the rain stopping. New York weather is so unpredictable.

"I live around the bend." She pointed. "Take a left."

After deciding to head to Long Lake, I admitted strange places make me uncomfortable. "Besides, this won't take all night." Minutes later, I steered the car into a deserted lane that Danny, my son, and I walk along. He's a good boy, a terrific fourth-grader.

Handing her a five, I assumed we wouldn't be seen. She quickly folded the bill and slid it down her front, in the cleavage.

Her smile lit up the darkness like a panther's grin. "Good, you can smile," I murmured, reaching for her. "Come closer." She jerked away. I approached her again. Hell, I just paid the woman to perform. There we were, in the middle of nowhere, the water some fifty feet in front of us, me anticipating, her not budging. Without thinking, I grabbed her hair and pulled. Her head hit the dash and mighty hard. The sound penetrated the silence. Cowering against the door, she told me to leave her alone. Then she opened the door and fled. Yards from the car, her black heel got stuck in the mud. I swear that's how it happened, and the next thing I knew, she tumbled and cracked her skull on a boulder.

Stalked by the moon, she never saw the rock. I didn't spot it either. To tell you the truth, I didn't notice much, listening to my heartbeat, but the sight of a dead woman sticks out like a red sky at night.

Alone with my thoughts, I trembled. What will Dee think? And the children? Their lives, my career, the finances? We'll lose the house. As my mind ran away, I watched blood spurt from her ears. I vomited on the dirt road and my imported loafers.

I stood in the mud, staring into the blackness. Leaving her wasn't an option. I'm a good person. I have a great reputation.

My chest heaved when I dragged the ankles. You can never understand how I felt, stumbling along the sand, trying to maintain balance on mushy underground, hauling a corpse behind me.

Begging the Lord for fresh air, I felt my palms sweat, but I kept creeping along the grapevine-shrouded beach, panting. Less than a hundred feet in front of me, an overturned rowboat greeted us. "Thank you, God," I said.

My common sense intact, I decided to take her across the lake. I wanted to maintain some sense of her dignity. Not that she had any, mind you. The kid was selling her body to the night for five dollars, a cup of coffee and chocolates.

Kneeling in the sand, I asked for forgiveness. "This was never meant to be," I said to the open evening. Then, with all the energy I could muster, I turned the dingy right-side up.

Rowing was difficult. I put in sixty hours that week and crammed myself full of coffee to stay awake. Mid-week my hands shook. My secretary thought I had Parkinson's disease, but they leveled out. I was tired. Too tired to think, too tired to concentrate. I swear it was an accident! A dreadful accident!

A hundred feet from shore, the boat tipped. I watched her go under. The five-dollar bill floated, and I grabbed it. What else could I do but swim?

If it weren't for lousy luck, I wouldn't have any. A man walking his poodle witnessed the incident. They found me at Sparky's, drinking coffee. Soaked from head to toe, I worried about pneumonia. People die from it, you know.

A day later, they took my Coupe Convertible. They never bothered to handle the beauty with care, and I specifically instructed, "Be careful with my baby." The hood is scratched. I told Dee to find someone to repair it.

Phil Noonan, the strapping warden, stood outside my cell. "What shall I order before they melt your flesh?"

Familiar eyes pierced mine, and I wanted to ask why he is mean. Society's majority never used to be mean. Sure, every so often, you might meet a straggler, someone who has always been mean, but not many people were mean when I was growing up. Now, they are downright rotten to the core.

"I would appreciate a bag of chocolate and a cup of coffee," I stated. "A big cup if possible."

"Do you have anything to say or ask?"

Face to face with the maniac, I asked her name. Frightfully worried, I forgot her name.

The warden reached through the bars and put his big hands on my shoulders. "Laura Jean."

"Oh, yes. Pretty girl. I wonder if she could swim."

Iron-like hands choked me. I breathed hard, heavy, to stay conscious.

"Laura Jean Noonan!" the warden yelled. "She was my niece!"

I wonder if the Governor will pardon me. I have a good reputation.

10
Hail Mary

Photo by Marlon Paul Bruin

In a small, wainscoted room, holding a photograph, Margaret wept. Saliva drooled from the sides of her mouth. An amber bottle rolled from the young novice's skirt, spilling its final drops onto the floor.

"Sister Margaret!" Sister Rosalie yelled. "What have you done?" Rosalie tripped on the braided rug, lunging for the empty bottle. She ignored the chocolate bar wrapper beside it. "Our Father, help us!"

"He loved me, and I him," Margaret whispered, collapsing on the pumpkin pine floor. "It's over."

Rosalie jammed a finger into Sister Margaret's mouth. "What's this nonsense you 'loved him'?" she asked, shoving her middle finger deeper, gagging the despondent woman. "You gave your life to God! Spit it out! Give up the poison!"

Spilling bile and toxins, Margaret gurgled, "They made me." Then she slipped into the darkness.

It's true. Margaret's parents, more so her mother, initiated her stay at the abbey. Mary did not approve of Teddy McBride.

"I hear what you are saying, Margaret, but Teddy is not like our family," Mary had said, pouring tea. "He's, well, a simple boy. And the last thing this family needs is a simple boy ruining our fine blood line."

Nineteen-year-old Margaret reached for her cup of tea. "I love Ted, and I know he'll make a good husband."

Pushing a wisp of hair settled on an eyebrow aside, wife of Vincent Curley, M.D. objected. Mary insisted the McBride boy wouldn't fit in. "He's different. You'll be forced to work, and you'll age quickly."

Margaret sipped tea. *Maybe Ted's not the one, but I love him. I want to carry his children!*

"You only think you love him," Mary said, spooning extra sugar into

52

the delicate cup. "Your father and I don't approve. After all, what would people say about the doctor's daughter marrying a plumber? Ha!" Waving a linen napkin, Mary had heard enough.

"But we'll leave the area. I promise." *But I adore this town.*

"Yes, you will leave town and put this behind you," Mary said. Her mother's angry threat: *Mary, you will marry the doctor or you will lose every cent we saved for you*, abruptly entered her head. "Your father and I are sending you to the abbey."

"'The abbey'?" Margaret tipped her cup. "But I don't want to be a nun!"

"You used to, Margaret." Stubborn, Mary poured tea. "And there's no sense forfeiting your dream to a plumber."

"He's a good man, Mother"—*Maybe she's right*—"and we love each other." *Maybe I should be a nun. Once, I wanted to be. I love Ted.* Pinching her heavy eyelids, Margaret asked for more tea.

Combing a checkered alley cat's spine, Elaine stressed, "You and Ted love each other. Why the change of heart?"

"I'm confused," Margaret said, tightening her grip on the Captain Kid Cola bottle. "I hope I'm doing the right thing."

"Going to an abbey isn't going to help. Move in the second-floor apartment. Ike won't mind." Poking her belly, Elaine admitted, "When the baby comes along, I'll need help."

"I can't," Margaret said, then thought, The junkyard across the way, the paper factory, and trash everywhere. I should stay. This is my mother's fault. She's never cared about me. Don't be silly, Margaret. You're acting abnormal. Something's wrong with your head. You'll make a fine nun, a woman you're father and I will be proud of… You can't disgrace this family and marry Ted, Margaret. What would the neighbors say? They'll crucify your father and I. Think of his practice. "Thanks, but I can't stay with you and Ike."

Feeling as if rats crawled along her limbs, Margaret shifted positions, crossing her legs, uncrossing them a few seconds later. Wanting to be home, Margaret believed Ted deserved a few minutes of her time. Halfheartedly, and against her mother's wishes, she sat with him in Brickman's ice cream parlor, pouring chocolate syrup over vanilla ice cream. "It will never work out, Ted." *I still love you.* "Things don't always work out"—*No, you don't…a fine nun.*

"We love each other," Ted said, reaching for her hand. Margaret pulled it away. "What happened to you? Why the freeze?"

"Stop making a spectacle of me!" *Mother said this would happen; he will bring you down!* "I'm leaving in two days, and that's that!"

It would have annoyed Ted's father to see his son loitering on the hood of a rusted truck in front of Jackson's Country Store, but Ted didn't think about family. A man in love, he worried about Margaret, and he wondered why she changed her mind. They dated for six months, and he never saw signs of her drifting.

After nine long days without her mother and the teakettle constantly steaming, Margaret felt physically drained. Thinned out, with her adrenaline decreased, she felt weak.

Margaret understood that no matter how pleasant she acted, smiling on the outside, bawling inside, she didn't belong in the cold building, or with the religious women. She thought, this is my mother's fault. She's never cared about me. She only cares about herself, but I love my mother very much. What did I do to be sent away? I tried to make her happy. Why can't she love me? Doesn't my mother love me?

The young woman knew she was at the abbey because she agreed with her mother, to keep Mary happy. When Mary was happy— everyone was supposed to be happy. And when Mary was upset—Mary expected her family to rally. And rally they did, to shut Mary up.

Her natural state poked through the chemical fog, but Margaret didn't realize it. She had never questioned her sanity.

Margaret praised God, loved all people, and desired world harmony, but she wanted Ted and children, too. She considered herself desperate, trapped at the abbey, sentenced to a miserable future.

With her head eliminating poison, torn between her mother's desires and her feelings for the plumber, Margaret wandered the dark hall, hoping the women slept deep. Eager to abandon chipped walls and ominous surroundings, she spotted the iron latch.

Trepidation mounted and her adrenaline rose. Margaret crept along the rocky walk, in the mist, praying. Quickly snipping *Hail Mary*, her mind pulled her back to Ted. Her mind always returned to Ted.

Though difficult for Ted to accept the breakup, he knew his life must go on. Having lost his brother to a fire, he knew his time was precious. Pulling a Wrigley's stick from his coat pocket, Ted watched the horses in the coral, next to Mr. Jackson's store, and considered his future.

Suffering from delusions, brought on by worrying increasing cortisol and adrenaline—and the chemicals altering her brain function— Margaret decided to end her life. Seeing a high rock in the mucky water surrounding the abbey, she hiked her nightgown, then wandered into the bay. Tepid, dirty water toyed with her, like her emotions. She waded.

"Anybody home?" Ted shouted, entering Jackson's store.

"Back here."

Not recognizing the pleasant voice, Ted looked down aisles for its owner. At the end of the third aisle, dipping a measuring cup into a flour sack, Samantha smiled. A red bandana held her bangs in place. Admiring the little doll, Ted wondered if he was dreaming. He asked for Mr. Jackson.

"My grandfather took ill," Samantha said, scooping flour. "They sent for me yesterday. Do you need eggs?"

Though on his list, eggs didn't mean anything to Ted. Removing the lid from a green jar, he mentioned a pack of Lucky Strikes. His smoking had picked up since Margaret left.

Pulling weeds from her shins, the sleep deprived woman thought the water too shallow, and she believed herself too weak to take her final breaths under a death pond. Like the wind shifts direction, Margaret changed her mind. Clenching her jaws, she turned toward shore, determined to undo the fiasco and marry Ted.

Mary smiled, acknowledging the couple in St. Paul's church. Ted and Samantha sat in the eighth row.

Genuflecting at the fifth row, Mary whispered, "Hail Mary!"

"I'll have to write Margaret," Mary stressed. "Don't you agree?"

"Let it go," Dr. Curley advised, but no matter what he said Mary did as she pleased. Unwilling to feed Mary's icy fires, Dr. Curley thought about Giselle, his secret friend.

Desperate for comfort, reading, "They looked lovely together, so caring and," Margaret wanted to return to the womb, to begin again, but after the womb spit her out its proprietor closed shop and tended to her own needs rather than her daughter's. She opened her nightstand drawer and reached for a Cadoo chocolate bar. Anticipating solace, she ripped the wrapper, broke the bar, and stuffed half in her mouth. Without delay, she slipped into a psychoactive state, full-blown mania.

This isn't happening! It can't be real! At first, Margaret wanted to jump out of her skin and flee. Suddenly she thought about getting into bed and staying there. *Dear God! Help me, God! I can't live without Ted! I can't live!* Her limbs burned as she paced the room. *I don't want to live anymore!*

"He will marry her," the letter informed. "Kay Smith informed me they go everywhere together…Your father and I are selling the house. We decided that a smaller place will…"

Stuck! I'm stuck here! Swallowing the last bite of chocolate, Margaret ran to the tool shed, climbed a water-warped ladder and searched the shelves. *Linseed, grass seed… I can't live! Nobody knows I'm alive! No one cares! I'm not alive—I'm dead, dead, oil, turpentine, liquid arsenic! I can't live!*

"Dear, Kay says they're going to Europe this fall," Mary remarked, peeling potatoes. "I've always wanted to go to Europe. Do you think we can visit France soon? I also need to see the breathtaking flower arrangements and little, painted windmills in Holland. Kay says…"

Vincent's eyes never left the newspaper. Listening to the phone ring, he told his wife to answer it.

The cold parlor overflowed with visitors saying their farewells. Lilies, roses and Novena cards couldn't warm the room, for the young lady had passed too soon.

"It's too soon," Mary said, holding a pink hankie under her nose.

Extending a hand, Ted said, "I loved her, too, Mr. Curley."

"And she you," Dr. Curley quietly stated.

Leaning on her husband, Mary quipped, "Then you should have married her, Ted. Margaret was never meant for the nunnery."

11
The Forrester House

Oregon Reform School, circa 1907

Excessively hairy, from head to chin, the dark-skinned mechanic stated, "The brakes are shot." Sliding a greasy rag along the front bumper, Ollie claimed the aged Pontiac wouldn't make it.

"What will my sister say?" Noreen asked, stomping her feet. "We always spend Easter together."

"Mrs. Manning, if you take the car, it may be your last Easter."

Unfolding a dollar bill, Calvin assured his mother that Ollie would fix the car. "I'm going to get a tonic. Want one?"

"There he goes, telling me what to do again!"

"He's right, Mrs. Manning. I'll have the car back in no time."

Comfortable in the living room, knitting Stella a white sweater, Noreen thought about dinner. Despite his constipation and fever, Calvin had served ham, mashed potatoes, salad and coffee. "You did a fine job, Calvin!" Noreen yelled. Washing the dishes, Calvin nodded, waiting for the follow-up. "Stella cooks the potatoes longer, but lumpy potatoes are okay. They get the system going."

Watching rain spit against the windows, Calvin heard a thump. It repeated, scaring him. "Mom, I think someone's outside!"

Don't be ridiculous." *Knit, pearl.* "You're always hearing things. Who would be out in this rain?" *Knit, pearl. Idiot son of mine.*

Bang! Clunk! "Move it, Joe!"

Dashing into the living room, Calvin perspired. He insisted that something stirred outside the house.

"Don't be absurd. Get me some more coffee, will you?"

At an early age, Calvin became responsible for helping his mother. "Calvin!" she cried, in the middle of the night. "Your father's hitting me!" Six-year-old Calvin climbed out of bed, ran to the master bedroom, and hollered at his father to leave his mother alone. With his hands, he covered his eyes, hoping the scene would go away.

"Go back to bed, idiot!" Ralph slugged Noreen again, hard, on her jaw. "You can't save her! This is between your mother and I!"

That was a long time ago, and the couple divorced when Calvin was eight years old, but the damage lingered. Conditioned, Calvin tried being the man of the family. Chronically stressed from the pressure of it all, his nervous system rocketed out of control.

"You'll never be the man of the family," Noreen cackled. "Look, Stella. He's taking the trash out." Worn out, thirteen-year-old Calvin ignored his mother. He lifted the heavy bag and dragged it across speckled gray linoleum. Noreen opened another beer, her tenth that day.

"Fool, the bag is leaking!" Noreen hung over her son. "When you're done, grab the mop!"

"Leave him alone, Mom!" Two years Calvin's junior, Stella shoved her piggybank aside and ran to her room.

"But he'll never be the man. Will he, Stella?"

Memories drifted in and out of Calvin's head as he washed the last pot, but noises interfered with his thoughts. "Mom, something's wrong. I hear odd sounds."

"It's in your head!" *Knit, pearl. Stupid schizo boy of mine.* "Any dessert tonight?" *Knit, pearl.*

Pouring cola, Calvin mentioned a box of chocolates.

"You know I like real dessert. Do I have to come out there and make myself pudding?"

Ignoring his mother, determined to find the root of the noise, Calvin drank cola. Pulling a checked curtain aside, to see what was going on outside, he wanted to cry. The teenager observed blackness.

The stove sparkled and the sink glistened, but Noreen focused on three onion peels littering the floor. "You're irresponsible!" she shouted. "Stop looking out the window! There's nothing out there, but there's garbage on my floor!"

"There's something going on outside!" Calvin shouted, trembling. "I know there is!" He closed the curtain.

"Don't you raise your voice at me!" Noreen searched the cupboard for pudding mix. "I'll have you thrown into the reform school. How would you like that?"

"Mom, listen. I didn't do anything wrong."

"Did you take your pill?"

"I took the damn phenothiazine. Okay?"

"Vulgarity is not accepted in my home!" Noreen yelled, yanking the eggbeater from under the sink.

"I can't take it anymore."

"Of course, you can't, because you're wacko. I thought you'd beat the odds, but the psychiatrist told me that people with your condition have breakdowns easily. You must have inherited it from your father's family. They have poor genes." Noreen waved the eggbeater. "They're coming to get you! The invisible people will crash through the windows any minute."

"Stop it, Mom. You're not funny."

Clank! Clunk!

"See? You must've heard that!"

"I'm calling the doctor, Calvin, and ruining his Easter, too, because there's nothing out there, and I've about had it with you! There's something wrong with your head!"

Dr. Franks encouraged Noreen to calm down. "Maybe Calvin needs the Forrester House," he said. "Seventeen is a difficult age, and from what you've told me, your son needs more discipline. It may help him in the long run, his lack of ambition from the schizophrenia."

"Yes, you're right, Dr. Franks," Noreen said. She asked the psychiatrist to meet them at the reform school the next day.

Pouring Black Lightning Cola, Calvin informed his sister their mother was sending him away. Then he asked, "What can I do? I've been trying to please Mom forever, but no matter what I do, it's never good enough, Stella. What can I do?"

Concerned about her brother, Stella reassured, "It's not you, Calvin. We both know it's Mom. She's a bitter woman who doesn't want anyone to be happy."

Subject to ongoing dysfunction, Calvin almost believed any place might be better than home. Confused, he stuffed black socks into a paper bag, wondering how to please his mother.

Fed up with the routine, Stella confronted their mother. "What are you thinking about, sending Calvin to the Forrester House? Mom, he's a good son and a great brother!"

Noreen didn't listen, wouldn't bring herself to accept the truth. In a caffeine-induced mental haze, similar to her son's caffeine-induced clouded state, she stormed into the living room, sat down, and threw the knitting needles. They hit the mantelpiece and fell to the floor. "Maybe you should go somewhere, too!" Noreen yelled. "You're a little tramp!"

Flustered, Stella ran into her room. She slammed the door.

"We'll take the silver."

"Maybe there's jewelry."

Forget it. It's in your head. Momma knows I'm wacko. Calvin pulled the light string.

Signing the admittance form, Dr. Franks remarked, "Thirty days is good, Mrs. Manning. Calvin may appreciate this one day."

"Maybe, but it seems strange that the only other person in the Manning and Day families who acts crazy is my sister-in-law, Becky."

"Then it seems your son must've inherited the schizophrenia from your husband's side," Dr. Franks claimed. "His paranoia, the voices, disrespect and anger clearly signify your son's progressed state."

As Calvin read *Life* in the sleeping quarters, Stella dined with friends at Zee's Pizza joint and Noreen chatted with Dr. Franks, the Balonski brothers stuffed Noreen's silver candlesticks into white pillowcases. They escaped the neighborhood with more than $5,000 worth of antiques.

12
Shades of Gray

Photo by J.R. Goleno

A World War II army veteran, Rudolph Baker suffered mentally. His wife also suffered, coping with Rudolph's problem. But the affluent couple considered themselves lucky. Rudolph balanced books for the state, they owned a four-story brownstone in Queens, their bedroom set, wingchairs and sofa came direct from Uptown Furniture's window, and their children were prime students. Still, the problem persisted. Flashbacks.

They're coming! Get down! Duck! Sweat seeped from Rudolph Baker, soaking the sheets. *Right there, next to you, the enemy!* Panting, Rudolph rolled onto his side and reached for the woman's long, red hair.

Half awake, staring into her husband's lost eyes, Marilyn gasped. Tight around her neck, burly hands choked her. Clawing, she struggled to free herself. "Rudolph, stop!" Marilyn mumbled. "It's me. You're home!"

"Uh, oh. Oh, oh!" Rudolph released Marilyn's neck. Screaming, "Jesus, forgive me!" he woke their three children. Marilyn looked in on them before retiring for the second time.

"Shell-shock," Dr. Quale diagnosed Rudolph Baker. "It happens to servicemen. There's not much anyone can do about it."

"Do you think diet is involved?" Rudolph asked. For relief and solid sleep, the good man would've changed anything, including his eating habits.

"We don't drink liquor, Dr. Quale." Admiring herself in the mirror by the door, Marilyn touched her hair, adorned with a tortoise shell barrette. "We never have. But we do like our coffee."

The doctor claimed diet is not involved with shell-shock. "It seems to be a combination of bad nerves and gene malfunction. Something might've happened in the war to change genes. Check back with me next month, Rudolph," Dr. Quale said, turning the glass doorknob. "Maybe you'll feel better by then."

At The Landing, an upscale Italian-American restaurant, Rudolph ordered swordfish, Marilyn the veal. Rudolph asked for their favorite beverage, thick Banjo Coffee, murky enough to stand cactus in. Believing it strange the couple drank coffee before dinner, Marissa, a stocky waitress, chuckled, knowing they would stay alert longer than they wanted to. I suppose anything goes, Marissa thought.

Pouring coffee, Marissa noticed a lady in a gray suit rush by her, on the way back from the powder room. *The war is over, but anything goes.*

"Is your father really a Yale supporter? After all, he's from Newton, and Newton houses Harvard graduates." Marilyn wanted to know, to convince Rudolph Jr. to attend his grandfather's choice school.

Distracted, Rudolph ogled the woman in gray. At the table across from them, she tapped a silver cigarette case, keeping pace with the phonograph music, streaming from the bar. Tailored to fit, her suit trimmed with gold buttons disturbed Rudolph. "He's a Yale fan." Tap, tap, tap. "A Yale supporter," Rudolph said, and suddenly clenched his teeth, hoping the noise ceased.

Marilyn looked at the woman tapping and drinking champagne. The thin brunette's hair was pinned in a bun, and gray laceups stopped above her ankles, almost to the shins.

Tap, tap—*One, two, pop, pop, pop!* Tap, tap, tap. *Three, four, fall in!* Haunted, Rudolph sipped coffee.

"She's quite loud," Marilyn said, but decided not to stare.

Lost in the past, Rudolph assured Marilyn the noise didn't bother him. *There, in the corner!* Tap, tap! The pink faded from Rudolph's cheeks.

"Honey, are you all right?" Marilyn steadied her husband's hands.

Move up, men! Watch your step! Tap, tap, tap! *There, over there, the enemies! Pop, pop! We're smoking! Quick—Sergeant Verone is down! Watch the fire!* Rudolph grabbed the tablecloth, bringing the floral centerpiece and lightly stenciled china to the floor. Perceiving all patrons as soldiers, the mentally disjointed man dove under the table.

The woman in gray reached for Marilyn, to comfort the distraught wife. Marilyn backed up, asking the woman to leave, but she ignored her. "Please," Marilyn insisted. "He'll be fine."

Abruptly lashing, Rudolph viciously attacked the woman's shins with broken glass, convinced he prevented her from harming his wife, who he perceived as a nice woman. Blood soaked through gray material.

"Someone, get help!" A patron ran in circles. "The man is mad!"

Whispering, dinner guests crowded the table. Marilyn pleaded, requesting the strangers leave the scene.

The Landing's owner and manager, Santo Marseppi, ordered Rudolph to come out. Huddled in a fetal position, Rudolph ignored Santo's orders. "Come out or I'll call the cops, you son of a bitch!"

"I'm very sorry. I'm sorry. This is so unlike Rudolph, but my husband was in the service." Marilyn wept. "He has shell-shock. There's nothing we can do about it."

"Tell that woman's lawyer!" a stranger retorted.

"No, no lawyer," the woman in gray stated, dabbing a lace-trimmed handkerchief against Marilyn's cheek. "My father was in the army, and I know what you're going through."

"It's me, honey." Marilyn led Rudolph out from under. "It's okay. Let's say goodbye to these lovely people and go home."

"Have a shot of Scotch," the woman in gray advised. "Sometimes it takes away bad memories."

The evening after the episode, humiliated, frustrated, and angry about his condition, Rudolph sat in his office, drinking black coffee. Desperate to feel normal again, he considered Bud Webber's invitation. "It's only a game or two," Bud had said, delivering legal papers. "Meet us there if you want."

"I'm going to meet the boys, Marilyn." Rudolph stretched the black phone cord. "Bud invited me to the Dryboard."

Slipping from Bud's hands, a pen fell to the floor. Rudolph's heart sped. *Here it comes! I can feel it!*

"What are you drinking, Baker?" Turnip, thick-skinned, like the vegetable, reached for the deck of cards.

I've got to get out of here! You'll look like a weirdo. Two days in a row. Coffee. At least stay for a cup. "Any coffee around?" Rudolph asked.

"'Coffee'?" Turnip shuffled the deck. "Coffee's for women."

Have a shot of Scotch. Sometimes it takes away... "Any Scotch?"

"Now you're talking!" Bud grabbed his cigarettes from the table.

"It's late and you smell," Marilyn said, in the hall, staring at the grandfather clock, approaching two o'clock. "Were you drinking? Because we agreed not to a long time ago."

Have a shot of Scotch. "Stop it, right now!"

"Don't be fresh with me! We've both had a long day." Marilyn climbed the stairs. "You, stay on the sofa."

Calming down, Rudolph inquired about dinner. He missed the meal.

"Roast pork and potatoes."

Ill at ease in the living room, Rudolph dined alone, drank a cup of coffee, and ate a handful of chocolate-covered nuts. Then he prayed for solid sleep.

Waking to the sound of his son flushing the upstairs toilet, Rudolph fell from the sofa. *He's there, Baker, in the grass. The enemy... They're all around us! Bang! Pop, pop, pop! Crawl, now, go!* Darkly dazed, soaked in perspiration, Rudolph reached for the dinner knife on the table.

Coming down the stairs, Rudy spotted his father crawling across the hall. "Dad, are you okay?" Deep into himself, fearing his son attacking him, Rudolph abruptly stood. "Dad, everything will be fine."

"Get out of your father's way!" Marilyn ordered. Breathing heavy, her arms whipping the air, she ran down the stairs, warning Rudy to stay away from his father.

Spying Rudy advancing, Rudolph stood. *The goal is to destroy the enemy before he destroys you. Do you understand?*

"Rudolph, it's me," Marilyn gingerly said, in the dark, approaching her husband. Pointing the knife at his son's chest, Rudolph backed Rudy against the sofa. "Honey, put the knife down," Marilyn instructed. "We're your family. We won't hurt you, Rudolph."

Struggling to stay on his feet, the young man toppled backward, onto the couch. "Rudolph, it's Rudy!" Marilyn screamed.

Marilyn grabbed the telephone, watching the madness progress. Hovering over his son, Rudolph plunged the knife into Rudy's chest. *It's him, the enemy! Baker, get him!* In another dimension, Rudolph wildly stabbed his son, unwilling to release the knife.

"It's my husband," Marilyn informed a police officer. "He's gone mad! He's stabbing our son!"

Rudolph dragged Rudy by the hair. "March on, soldier!" he ordered. "Be proud!" Bleeding profusely, Rudy slid along the floor.

Rudolph wept. "I killed our child, Marilyn. My condition finally broke me. May God forgive me. I can't live like this any longer. I killed our Rudy, Marilyn." Howling hysterically, Marilyn cradled their son.

"Your husband experienced a psychotic break," Dr. Quale claimed. "Something inside him went haywire. The good doctors at the asylum are treating him."

Surrounded by green walls, Marilyn asked what really happened.

"He had a psychotic episode," Dr. Quale insisted.

"But that's never happened before. My husband had a few bad dreams, nightmares, where he grabbed me, but Rudolph would never intentionally harm anyone. What happened was an accident."

Unsympathetic, Dr. Quale said, "I'm not convinced of that, Mrs. Baker. The subconscious is a strange thing. I know of cases where a patient seems fine one minute, and the next he beats his dog or throws his child across the room."

"But what instigates it?"

"Something in the brain goes wrong," Dr. Quale claimed. "No one knows why."

"I'm sorry, but I can't accept that. You're a psychiatrist, a medical doctor. You must know why. What happens? Why was my husband fine one minute and crazy the next?"

"Doctors don't know why, Mrs. Baker."

"But you said shell-shock 'happens to servicemen.' You said, 'There's not much anyone can do about it,' but you never mentioned the possibility of my husband killing one of our children."

"I did say that," Dr. Quale admitted, "but many veterans develop psychosis, too, and that's what happened to your husband. I presume his genes went astray."

"How? How can his genes go bad?"

"We don't know yet, Mrs. Baker. Please. Try to calm down."

"Dr. Quale, schizophrenia does not run in our families, and my husband is college-educated, with a good job. How did this happen?"

"Dr. Prescott at the asylum says Rudolph should start feeling better with the phenothiazine."

"How did this happen?" Marilyn asked. "How!" Waiting for a reasonable explanation, she stared at the man's icy eyes. Dr. Quale appeared vacant, as if he looked through the good woman.

Focused on the wall clock, the physician closed Rudolph Baker's folder. "The medical society does not have all the answers, Mrs. Baker. Let's talk again before the trial. In the meantime, I'll prescribe something for you to sleep."

13
The Number Nine

Courtesy of J. M. Sawyer

"More coffee, Father?"

Nora didn't wait for an answer. Pouring coffee, Mrs. Delaney complained, "It snowed for five days. Can you imagine? The angels were against us," *and they're still against me. This has been going on too long. I can't take it! Everyone is talking, whispering about me!* "Such a horrid storm."

"Now, Nora. You must think of something positive."

"How can I, Father? Maurice left after dinner and didn't return for hours." *He's cheating. I know he is.*

"That's no reason for you to get upset." Lifting his cup, Father Motherly advised, "Find out where he went in the snow."

"But I asked, Father." Nora passed the silver candy dish. "He said he went for a walk. 'A walk'! It's been too cold out there to walk!" *The only place he walked to was another woman's home—to keep warm in her bed!* Tears abruptly surfaced. "I'm sorry, Father, but Maurice is shaming the Delaney name."

Consuming a minimum of four cups of coffee a day and craving chocolate, panicky and paranoid, Nora had divorced her self. And married thirty years, she forgot about her anniversary.

Every year, Maurice surprised his wife. For their twenty-ninth anniversary, he handed the emotional woman a set of silver platters. The year before, he draped a pearl bracelet on her wrist. Wanting to make their thirtieth special, Maurice trudged through a snowstorm to meet his sister at Sherburne's Jewelry store. Studying the diamond in the window, he admitted, "I never could afford one, but Nora always wanted one. A kind woman, Nora never complains."

Slipping the ring on her finger, Colleen said it was too big. "Nora's fingers are delicately thin."

"It will take a few weeks to size it, Mr. Delaney. With the holiday season upon us, we're behind," Owen Sherburne said, polishing the ring. "You can pay for it, and I'll have it ready in a few weeks."

Maurice agreed, "That sounds fine." *Nora will rub my neck, asking what I bought for our anniversary. Such a good woman, an angel, she is. My pride and joy.*

"Maury shamed us. Married a Swede. That brought heartache, but my son didn't care. He refuses to visit."

Tired of listening to problems not affecting him, Father Motherly cleared his throat, and said, "My sister married a Swedish fellow."

Nora spit coffee into her napkin. Through the linen, she mumbled, "You don't have to tell anyone, Father. I'll keep your secret."

"Oh, it's no secret, Nora. Arthur is a wonderful man, a dedicated family man. They own the meat market in Newtal Square."

"My son's wife is a nurse," Nora said, wiping the table. "The nerve of her working all day." *I know he's cheating on me, Father. What will the neighbors say? First a Swede, then a divorce. What will I do?*

The priest knew Rita Barry would be worried. He promised to be at her house at one. It was half past. Standing, he said, "Thank you for the coffee and sweets, but I have to go. Rita is likely to flatten me with a bread roller if I don't show up soon."

Nora wiped her dry hands on a dishtowel. "Thanks for stopping by." *I am so humiliated!* "But what will I ever do?"

Father Motherly stressed, "God is with you."

"Yes, yes," *but angels break my bread, and the devil breaks my heart.*

Her eyes heavy from sleep deprivation, Nora peered through thick, beige curtains, watching the priest step into the black sedan. She thought, What does he know? Evelyn Hathaway will know, and that Partridge woman will laugh. They might all know, every one of them! Maybe it's one of them. I see the way they look at my handsome Maurice—with their roaming eyes. I can never face the ladies at church again! Mary, mother of God, help me!

Sipping coffee, Nora wondered about dinner: *Spaghetti and salad? We had that yesterday. For goodness sakes, it's Friday. I almost forgot the fish.*

Determined to surprise his wife, Maurice called Nora and mentioned running an errand. "I'll be home late."

Disoriented, Nora snapped, "What do you mean you'll 'be home late'? It's Friday. You always come home on time."

"I know, I know," Maurice rushed, "but tonight's special. I have to do something. Fix yourself some dinner and take a nice bath. I'll be home soon."

"Are you taking the Number 9?"

"Yes, honey. The Number 9."

"I have to pick up a loaf of bread. I'll meet you there."

"Nora, honey, stay home. It's cold out there."

"No, Maurice! I will meet you at the station!"

"Okay, then. Whatever makes you happy."

A damn blood bath! That's what I'll take! Nora removed her dark wool skirt, lilac blouse and cotton undergarments and stepped into the water.

Six minutes, seems like one hundred. I can't stay in here any longer. Sit still! Stand up! Get up! Run, Nora, run from it all before they know!

You're a sad excuse for a woman, Nora Delaney. A little more rouge might help. Dab it on! Help what? Who said that? Certainly pink cheeks won't bring him back. Do you hear the voices? They're near the window, people staring through you, reading your mind. Dear God, what did I do to deserve this? I've been a good wife, a good mother, a devoted Catholic... Nora's mind would not pause.

Look at you, all dressed and no place to go. Finish your coffee. That's it; soothe your insides before—Before what? Before the Number 9 rolls in carrying the low, lying cheater! Bless me, Father! They all know... First a Swede, then a whore. What a disgrace! Quick! Grab your coat! That's it— hurry your arms into it.

She walked fast, down Elm Street, turned onto Page, and hailed a taxi. "The North Station," Nora said, "and please hurry."

"Isn't it lovely, Dorothea?" Maurice asked, tucking the ring back into the box. "Nora will be very surprised."

"It's a fine piece, Maurice," the neighbor said, then she mentioned sweet potato pie. "I made it for dinner. Nora and you should stop over for a piece. Burt loves it."

"Maybe tomorrow, but tonight is special." Closing the little, satin-lined box, Maurice smiled.

Everyone is looking at me! "How much do I owe you?" *How dare they!*

"One dollar, twenty cents," the cab driver replied, opening his hand.

I wore my best dress, and my face is prettied up. God, help me, I never thought this day would come. Reaching for the wooden ladder, Nora felt her legs stiffen and heart race. *Man cheats on wife and wife does what she has to do. Mother of God, I'm the shame of the city! Look at everyone staring...*

On the platform, onlookers feared the situation. "One bad move might push her over," a stranger whispered to his wife.

"Don't go near her," a man cautioned his children.

A woman yelled, "There's a policeman!"

"Lady, don't go down there!" a sweeper shouted. "The third rail is alive!"

"I'm dead!" *A Swede, a cheater, no one cares about me!* Nora scrambled down the ladder, looked back, and sped to the tracks.

"Lady, wait!" a man yelled, following Nora down the ladder.

"The son of a bitch is on the Number 9! On his whore, on the run from me, on the go without a thought for his wife of twenty-nine years!" Nora skipped over two tracks. *I'm bathed, prettied up, dressed in my fine blue dress with the white collar,* "the one you like Maurice!"

"Holy hell!" a policeman hollered, rushing down the ladder as Nora approached the live rail. "Lady, stop! Lady, please stop!"

Speechless, watching the stranger linger on the tracks, the conductor grabbed the brake switch. Twelve passengers in the front tumbled. Maurice bounced, slamming his head against a window.

Spreading her arms like a bird in flight, Nora stepped on the third rail. Electricity surged through her, before the train hit her.

Maurice felt his bruised head. "It's our anniversary. I'm Maurice Delaney," he said, in shock. "Will you please find my wife, officer? Nora is supposed to meet me at the station. My wife should be here."

"Your wife is here, Mr. Delaney," the policeman said, waving the hearse on. "She's under the wheels."

14
Only Dreams

Photographer, Mike Dijital

"The Board will give you sixty dollars if you approve it, Mr. McIntyre. Think of all the seed you can buy." Drawing lines on a newspaper, Dr. Cohen cleared his throat.

Insisting, "A boy stole those chickens. My kids never took a thing from no one," Hank McIntyre, a skeletal farmer, pulled a Camel from the courtesy box on the psychiatrist's desk.

"Well, the judge didn't see it that way. He sentenced Ellen to thirty days in our place here, and obviously none too soon. According to my analysis, and from what the nurses tell me, your daughter is mentally ill."

Scratching his head, the good father disagreed. "There's no mental illness in my family. None in my wife's either."

"It has to start somewhere. It's clear that Ellen is demented."

Listening to Dr. Cohen, Hank wanted to speak with someone. His wife died during childbirth, leaving him with six children, newborn to thirteen years old. Feeling pressured, Hank needed a woman's advice.

"I'm going to be upfront with you. If you don't sign the paper, the committee has the right to go ahead with it, regardless." Offering a pen, Dr. Cohen pushed the consent form at Hank.

On the spring afternoon that a policeman escorted Ellen into the station, the fourteen-year-old minded her own business, skipping home from school, up the dirt lane. Behind her, the butcher's son, a year older than Ellen, whistled. Weaving along the road, Ellen ignored Whitey. As she neared Huckleberry Farm, Ellen slowed, admiring cows grazing in the pasture and chickens in a screened pen. Whitey stalked her. "Like those chickens?" he asked. "Because I'm gonna get me one."

Ellen told the wretched boy to leave the chickens alone. She added, "You can't keep hurting living things."

The Wednesday before, Whitey chucked a rock at a snapping turtle crossing the road. Witnessing him stone the innocent creature, Ellen begged him to stop. Hooting, Whitey threatened to bash a rock over Ellen's head. She ran home.

Whitey climbed the fence. "I'm gonna get a chicken," he said.

Remembering Mrs. Franklin saying, "Whitey is trouble," the studious ninth-grader passed Mr. Berry's row houses and kept going.

Whitey snapped a chicken's neck. Blood spurted from the mouth.

"What do you mean you 'weren't involved'?" Writing Ellen's statement, Dan Lawry continued, "Seems to me and the others, Mrs. McBride, Miss Halloway and Mr. Berry himself, you were the only one besides Justin Lake on that road between the time the chickens were stolen and found dead, and we all know Master Lake uses crutches."

"Miss McIntyre, it says here you took a handful of lemon balls from a glass container in Worthington's drugstore," Judge Marlow stated. Intimidating Ellen, the judge asked for an explanation. Ellen started speaking, but Judge Marlow interrupted, "Stick to the answers, young lady. Never mind. I've heard enough." Sliding thick-framed glasses along his nose, the judge recommended thirty days observation at Upstate New York Asylum.

Believing in fairness and his daughter, Mr. McIntyre never contacted a lawyer. A prime citizen, Ellen rarely got in trouble. The only crime she committed was taking lemon suckers for a very pregnant Mrs. Ornstein, vomiting on Lenox Street. Grateful for the girl's help, Sheila Ornstein thanked Ellen, entered the pharmacy, and paid for the container of suckers, unaware that Mr. Worthington sent a complaint to the station.

Ten-year-old Ellen was not required to plead her case because Mrs. Ornstein waddled up the road, entered the station, and supposedly cleared things with policeman Lawry. Setting aside his coffee cup, Officer Lawry called Ellen a fine girl. "An easy oversight," he stated. "I'll destroy Worthington's note."

Things would have been different had that happened. Instead, Officer Cleave found Mr. Worthington's note and logged the complaint.

After Lawry heard about the dead chickens, he wondered why an excellent student would trespass and steal. Drinking coffee, he flipped through the logbook and noticed Ellen had stolen lemon drops. Policeman Lawry never recalled his conversation with Mrs. Ornstein.

After wondering whether he should trade his wife's clarinet for legal services, Ellen's father considered the sentence and concluded that thirty days would quickly pass without consequence. What a trusting soul.

"This is the way we do things here," a nurse's aide remarked, shoving a sack dress at Ellen. "Put it on."

In the basement, Ellen shuffled along the corridor, passing locked cells. Hooked to her, Nurse Jackie explained, "They're housed below because they can't ever be released. Too mentally ill."

"What do they do all day?"

"Eat, defecate, scream, scratch the walls and pick their skin."

"No books or anything?" Ellen asked.

"Honey, last one got a book shoved it up his tail. I never saw anything like that except the mouse. A big guy stuck a five-inch rodent inside him. By the time we chained him down and dug our way to China, the furry creature was dead. I prefer stuffing cotton in the dead. At least I know what to expect. Take a left."

Ellen stopped short to eliminate an itch. Not expecting the teen to halt, Jackie tripped and slapped cement. "Bitch! I'll get you for that."

"But it was an accident," Ellen said, noticing Jackie's eyes water. *Like Whitey's eyes.*

"You were an accident, McIntyre!"

Jackie pushed the frightened girl into Dr. Ledin's office. "We're here, Erma, and it wasn't a fun trip. Get in that chair!"

Examining Ellen, Dr. Ledin asked, "What's wrong with you?"

"There's nothing wrong with me. Everything's a mistake." Ellen went on, explaining the situation leading to her admittance. Squeezing her hands, the doctor took in Ellen's beauty. Braided hair fell past her shoulders. Green eyes flickered life, and freckles zigzagged across a slender nose.

"No signs of psychosis," Ledin stated, offering Ellen a candy jar. Peppermint, lemon, and wintergreen balls kissed.

"Thanks, but I don't eat sweets. They're bad for good health."

"Delusional," Dr. Ledin reported. "Odd ideas about sugar."

"Mr. McIntyre," Dr. Cohen said, "the day after your daughter's admission, Dr. Ledin, one of the best, diagnosed Ellen as delusional. A young physician able to detect a delusional state will go far."

Relieved to be away from patients and caretakers, Ellen dangled her legs from the cot in Ledin's office, wondering why she sat there, answering the same questions. Fantasizing about feasting his hands on Ellen's flawlessness, Dr. Ledin had instructed an aide to escort Ellen to him every morning. Three days later, dawn breaking, a policeman accompanied Star Love, arrested for negotiating tricks for cash, into the asylum. Thrilled to exam Star, Dr. Ledin stopped obsessing about Ellen.

"Cut her hair," Nurse Bellows instructed an aide. Leaning back in her chair, the nurse grinned. "You say she refuses to eat pudding, won't touch cola or cinnamon-covered oatmeal—Then tie her down and cut that braid right off her head! We'll teach her to behave."

Not one to talk back, but concerned about Ellen's fate, Terry monitored her words. "Don't you think that's overdoing it?" she asked. "The girl just doesn't care for sugar."

"If I were you, I'd watch your mouth, Terry, because if you're not careful you may find yourself out of work without a reference." Standing, Bellows lit a cigarette.

Wearing a snug uniform, Nancy, a senior aide, approached the bed. Terry trailed. "We've a surprise, Ellen," Nancy insisted in her "Nothing's fair in this world" attitude. "You take her feet, Terry. I'll get the hands."

"I didn't do anything! Please stop!" Ellen begged the aides to leave her alone, but Nancy straddled her chest, determined to cut the braid.

"You didn't behave. I never did like long hair. Do you, Terry? You like long hair that took fourteen years to grow?"

Terry didn't utter a word until Nancy demanded she say something. With an out of work boyfriend, Terry recalled "You may find yourself out of work without a reference." She pushed "No" from her tongue.

Nancy pressed against Ellen's neck. Snipping at the base of the girl's head, she cut the braid off, puncturing Ellen's flesh. "You need medical attention," Nancy remarked, wiping a bloody finger on Ellen's face. "Good thing we've a nursing student here."

"She refuses to mingle and won't talk to Stacey, and those two seemed close," an aide reported. Twisting an elastic around her finger, Nurse Bellows ordered the young woman to lock Ellen in with Sadie.

Nauseous, Ellen contained her bile, rising in defense of biological odors. Sadie's cellar room reeked.

Swimming through Ellen's hair, crusted fingers rubbed her head. "Bye, bye, Birdie. I miss you, baby," Sadie sang, believing she comforted the teenager, who had intentionally tensed up and stopped talking.

Doctor Cohen said, "She's catatonic. Put her in a tub."

Ellen wasn't catatonic. She survived by shutting down.

"They took every tooth," Terry said, sponging Ellen's rigid neck. "Sadie bit off her grandson's fingers, and they brought her here seventeen years ago, escorted her to the dentist, and he pulled her teeth. Sadie no longer talks but sometimes, when I pass her room, I hear her sing." In the high tub, Ellen drew her knees close to her chest.

"Your daughter is non-responsive, Mr. McIntyre," Nurse Bellows said, on the phone, reaching for her cigarette pack. "I saw her myself. She's in a state of shock. It's best you return in a week."

"Give her some B12," Dr. Cohen instructed, handing Bellows a tourniquet. "She's bound to snap out of it."

Anxious to take a break, stepping on her Chesterfield, Nurse Bellows handed Terry a syringe. "You do it."

Dr. Ledin inquired about Ellen's diet, but her infection resulted from contamination, not a bad pear. Injecting Ellen with vitamin B12, Terry remembered she forgot to sterilize the needle. After Nurse Bellows asked about contamination, Terry lied, "I boiled the needle. Ellen must've caught Tilly's virus."

Hank greeted Ellen in a white room decorated with twenty cushioned chairs and healthy, green plants. Not knowing what to say, he claimed to like Ellen's haircut. Fearing what caretakers may do to her if she told her father the truth, Ellen smiled blankly.

With Ellen's natural smile misplaced, and her cheerful attitude absent, Hank questioned his daughter's mental state. She's acting strange, he thought, leaving the asylum. Maybe she is psychotic.

Before the town dragged her to hell, always in good spirits, Ellen treasured little people. She planned to teach school, marry, and bear five to six children. Society with its ludicrous beliefs robbed her.

"The money sounds good," Mr. McIntyre said, tucking a Lucky Strike into his hip pocket, "but I won't allow it. My daughter will be home tomorrow, and things will be fine. Like they used to be."

"It's your duty as a father to reconsider," Dr. Cohen urged, offering Hank a fresh box of cigarettes. He claimed, "Ellen is not normal."

"Normal or not, she's my kid, and I like her the way she is. I'll be back tomorrow, at noon sharp, to bring my daughter home."

"Thank you, Dr. Cohen, for trying," Sid Moraine, the asylum's director, said, "but the Board won't be responsible for the mentally ill procreating. If we send Ellen home in her state, we would be approving the cycle—A mentally ill woman begets a mentally ill child in far worse condition than herself. That child goes on to bring a sicker child into the world and so on. Before long, the world is full of loonies. We won't be responsible." Moraine pushed the consent form across the table. "All board members approved. Tomorrow morning, Dr. Stradford, a reputable surgeon, will sterilize Ellen McIntyre. She'll leave with her father at noon."

15
The Interrogation

Photo by Michael Connors

Handing Lester Coyle a paper cup full of coffee, Drew Lamont sternly questioned, "Why'd you shoot Bernie Salk, Lester?"

The oilman replied, "He shot at me first."

"Naw, he didn't, Lester. Bernie threw a rock. That's all. A little rock." Officer Lamont flipped his club and struck it against the table. "Then you shot him!"

"I saw it." Lester twisted his hands. "Bernie aimed and fired at me."

"A 'rifle'? Now, how could Mr. Salk walk up Bay Lane carrying a rifle—in broad daylight—and not one other person—and there were quite a few people on the lane this after, hanging laundry, planting petunias, playing hopscotch—witness Mr. Salk, mad as a bull missing mating season, with a rifle? He threw a rock! A pebble!"

"I don't mean to be disrespectful"—*My Lester is a good boy. Why, he can't harm a bee even if he wanted to*—"but the guy pointed the gun at me"—*My son didn't hit the Ryther boy. It never happened. Momma walked me home, she did.* "And so I got my rifle." Lester sniffed.

"Smells good, doesn't it?"

"Yes, sir," Lester said. "The coffee smells very good."

"Well, Lester, how would you like to smell piss and dung when you're in a cell?" The officer closed in, head to head. "Because that's what'll happen if you don't tell me the truth!"

"But I am! I am telling the truth!" *I told the truth, Momma. Honest I did. I'm so proud of you, son. Now, get your boneless spine up the lane!* "Don't beat me! Please—I'll be a good boy!"

"'A good boy'?" Officer Lamont asked, and snickered. "Where did that come from? You're a grown man. What are you talking about?"

Don't you be telling anyone our business. "Nothing. I'm sorry."

75

"Sorry for what, Lester? For shooting Salk? You're damn lucky he didn't lose bowel control, vomit in front of the Desmond kids, or blow an artery on the lane. You do know that, don't you?"

"Yes, sir. I'm lucky, very lucky," Lester said, tapping the coffee cup.

Beating a wall with his club, Officer Lamont ordered Lester to tell the truth. Familiar with lines, sob stories, and lies, he didn't plan on spending the night at the station pumping for information.

Lester swallowed hard. "I was on the porch, relaxing with my coffee and *Game and Reel* magazine, watching the neighborhood, when Bernie came up the lane, carrying a rifle. I slugged my coffee, rushed in the house, and found my gun.

'Son of a bitch!' Bernie yelled, running at me. 'Rhonda told me you flirted with her at the carnival! Is that right, you cowardly loser?'

I wasn't at the carnival, I swear! I told him as much, yelled back at the terror"—*I wasn't at the park, Momma. Honest, I wasn't!* — "but he didn't listen. Advancing, Bernie stood on my lawn and fired! I fired back. I didn't mean to kill him." Lester panted before bawling.

Snorting like a pig knee-deep in banana skins, Lamont couldn't contain his laughter. "'Ha, ha! Kill him'? Ha! You didn't kill anyone, so stop the pansy act. You hurt him though, bad. Bernie's at the emergency room, getting turned inside-out and stitched with hanger wire."

Before an EMT stabilized him, Bernie lost a half pint from the shoulder wound. In the ambulance, he moaned, "Can't get his own woman, so he goes after married women, women in the dumps."

"I hope he makes it." Lester's atom apple bobbed. "He will make it?"

"Sure, he'll make it. Bernie's a strong man, not like you weak son of a bitch!" Officer Lamont twirled the club and banged it against the wall. "Tell me what happened!"

I hit him, Momma, because he called you a poor man's whore, and I won't listen to that! You're good, Momma. It's the men, they're bad, not you. It's never you. In between sobs, Lester admitted shooting Bernie.

"We know that! Why! What happened?"

"He accused me of going after his wife at the carnival, but I wasn't there!" Lester half believed his half-truth. "I was with my brother. His truck needed plugs and tires." Lester looked at the door, then the counter. "We drank coffee, ate Myrna's brownies, fixed the car, drank some more, ate more, and then we parted."

"And then you went to the carnival?" Lamont held the pot. "More coffee? Is that what you're looking for?"

"Yes. No, no carnival."

Pouring coffee, Lamont said an officer found Lester's ticket.

Where did I hide it? Under my bed? In the refrigerator? Where? Think!

Officer Lamont picked up a paper lunch bag, crumpled it, and threw it at Lester. It scratched his nose.

Sticks and stones will break your bones… It hurts, Momma. Lester covered his face with his hands. "It was dark when I got home." *Don't let your boyfriend beat my face, please tell him to stop!*

"Look at me! That's not what Roger Bruno said. Roger said he saw you 'pull up around three.' You even said you were on the porch in the afternoon. Which was it? Day or night!"

Officer Netto cracked the door and poked his head into the room. "Change of shift. Want me to take over?"

"The only person taking over Lester will be a shrink. You're mental, Lester. Do you know that?"

Lester claimed there wasn't any mental illness in his family.

"Maybe it's the drugs." Officer Lamont slid his club into the holder. "Don't you use cocaine?"

"Never tried it"—*Because I'll kick you from here to kingdom come!*

"Amphetamine? I bet you like speed, don't you?"

"Never tried it"—*Because I'll bloody your hide!*

"Then you're a nut case, Coyle!" Officer Lamont said, hurrying to the door. "It's plain as that."

Tossing a cardboard box into the room, Officer Netto said Cell 6 was ready. "Clean and shiny, like a baby's bottom."

"Everything in," Lamont ordered. "Shoes, shirt, the whole nine yards. You'll be staying with us for the weekend, and going to court Monday."

Untying his sneakers, Lester asked to call a lawyer.

"You can make a call, Lester, only there's a little problem." Lamont chuckled. "Our phone is broken. We'll settle you in with another cup of coffee, and after breakfast you can make your call. How's that?"

"It sounds okay," Lester answered, knowing he didn't have a choice.

Officer Netto held a log sheet. "What's the deal?"

"Mentally insane. Smart enough, but a real loon bug."

"I've seen an increase in that lately," Netto said, raising his eyebrows. "It's awfully strange so many people are cracking up."

Lamont punched the time card. "You might want to give a head's up, Netto, because someone'll have to call the institute. I've a feeling this one's going away for a long time. Get him some more coffee, will you?"

16
Johnny's Red Wagon

Photo by J.M. Sawyer

The night before Christmas in the Davis home, Johnny prayed for a red wagon. There wasn't any reason the eight-year-old shouldn't have one. Except for throwing a chewed wad of spearmint gum at a neighbor's German shepherd, once, and swearing under his breath, the youngster was an all around child. An apple pie kid, some may say, but that Fisher boy, Johnny's first cousin? Carl was another story.

A naughty, restless boy, nine-year-old Carl spent the year teasing his classmates, throwing snowballs at neighborhood dogs, and annoying his mother with an incessant whine. Most people who knew Carl were accustomed to his noise.

As Carl begged, "All I want is a wagon," Sally ignored her son. "Mom, can't Santa or someone get me one. I didn't ask for anything else. Whhhy not?"

As expected, Johnny received a Radio Flyer. He found the wagon behind the tree, a gold bow dangling from its black handle. Carl received a pair of blue mittens, a box of chocolate Cadoo bars and Mr. Potato Head.

With tulips popping, Johnny retired wooden trucks, marbles and his Howdy Doody doll, and proudly pushed his Radio Flyer onto the side of the road. Carl strolled alongside, sipping a bottle of Captain Kid Cola, tossing pebbles into the wagon.

"Wouldn't it be neat for us to go to the frog pond?" Flushed with excitement, Carl hollered, "We can put frogs in the wagon!"

Wanting to keep the wagon clean, Johnny informed his cousin he didn't need any frogs in his wagon. Whining, Carl begged to go to the pond. Tired of the noise, Johnny turned the handle over to Carl.

Leading, Carl insisted, "There's nothing wrong with frogs."

"Yeah, but I like dogs better, even snakes. Frogs smell weird."

They sure do, and Johnny realized that more than ever, an hour later, pushing the wagon full of frogs up Hill Road.

"I can't bring them home," Johnny said. "My folks will kill me."

A grin confiscated Carl's face as the two trudged. He happily thought about Johnny's father whipping him, but his mood abruptly changed. Annoyed he didn't own a wagon, and had used his pulling time, Carl yanked a Choco-Bite box from his jacket pocket. Not bothering to offer Johnny one piece, Carl opened the box and popped the chocolate candies into his mouth. Within fifteen seconds, Carl thought about how cool it would be to see guts and blood spurt from little bellies. "Maybe we can kill them!" he said. "We can throw them at cars!"

Johnny watched Carl lift a three-inch frog. "That's not funny. Put it down!" And Carl did, in the center of Hill Road. As the boys watched a truck flatten the little fellow, Carl picked up another frog and threw it. Johnny called his cousin all sorts of names, but Carl didn't stop. In less than two minutes, he emptied the wagon. Hill Road was a mess.

One may think Johnny would have learned a lesson and avoided Carl, but that didn't happen. They were in the same class, and their mothers were sisters. Though the two grew apart mentally, they remained near.

"It's Johnny's twelfth birthday," Sally announced, uncomfortable on a thinly stuffed chair, darning a white sock. "We're going to your aunt's house tomorrow."

Relaxing on the sofa, as much as a teenager wired on Captain Kid Cola can relax, Carl asked what Rita and Edgar bought Johnny.

"A bicycle."

"Great. Whhhy does he get everything? It's not fair."

"Snap out of it, Carl. Someday maybe we can get you a bike, but you know how things are."

Yes, Carl knew the situation. The family was on the dole, with Carl's father out of work. "Your husband can't lift any longer," Dr. Townsend had warned Sally. "The job is too heavy on his heart."

"Nice looking bike, Johnny," Carl said, running his hands along the shiny handlebars. "Maybe we can pedal to Wilderness Dairy and get an ice cream sandwich."

"I dunno. It only has one seat."

"Aw, come awwwn. I can sit on the bars." Carl pushed back his overgrown bangs. "Todd and Billy cruise around town like that all the time. It's all right."

Changing the subject, Johnny mentioned cake. His mother spent the morning making a fudge cake and enclosing it in vanilla frosting.

Cake melted in his mouth when Carl reached for the Captain Kid bottle. Perspiring, he felt his heart race, but he didn't give it any thought. Besides, Carl was too young to drop like a lead balloon. Hyperactive, not realizing it, Carl stood and carried the bottle to the backyard.

"Get off my bike, Carl."

"Zoom, zoom! Hey, hop on the bars!"

Again, Johnny ordered Carl from the new bike.

"Let's go for a ride and come right back." Dilated eyes stared at the discouraged bike owner. "What do you say?"

"One drive down the road. That's it, and I'm pedaling."

"Come awwwn. You'll be pedaling this all over the place. Let me drive, once."

Sitting on the handlebars, Johnny grit his teeth. "Slow down, Carl!"

In the cola world of make-believe, Carl embarked on a delusional trip. *I can drive this new bicycle clear across the world—Faster, faster, faster! Maybe I can go to California—Remember the gold rush!* Forgetting to keep his eyes on the road, Carl looked around, savoring his pedal power. *Or to Plymouth, where the pilgrims landed! Maybe even Alaska!* The bicycle swerved from the side of the road into the traffic lane.

Cruising down the slope, Johnny spotted oncoming cars. With a madman pedaling behind him, he wanted to jump but knew he would hurt himself. White knuckling, he pleaded for Carl to slow down.

Faster, faster, faster! Side to side, Carl's eyes moved frantically, as he assessed the neighborhood, whizzing by them. *Look at the puppy! Oh hell! Turn the handlebars—I can't! Johnny's too heavy!* While the animal crossed their path, Carl steered the bicycle off the road and into a tree.

One Christmas Santa brought Johnny a Radio Flyer. For three years, he pulled it across town, to the pond, into the woods, and to Wilderness Dairy, where he bought ice cream. Johnny's mother and his aunt also used the wagon. After loading it with purple irises, they tugged it to St. Michael's Cemetery, where Johnny and Carl rest, side by side.

17
The Green Café

Photo by J. M. Sawyer

Nothing special, with banners taped to the window, and the outside needing paint, the one-room building welcomed young men. Every thirty minutes or so, an older man wearing a uniform and carrying a briefcase left the building and entered Green Café, next door. Every so often, a young man strolled from Green Café, entered the station, and signed his name. Each recruit believed in the promise of a brighter tomorrow.

Saving to buy a blue Mustang convertible, Dennis Leighton frosted donuts, served sandwiches and beverages, and took out the trash at the café. Wanting to ban recruiters, he believed in college, roaring waterfalls, Wrigley's peppermint, Rock 'Em Sock 'Em Robots and other priceless treasures life offered.

According to Dennis, war had no place in America, America had no place in war, and grown men had no right approaching teens and vagabonds while they sipped a beverage or devoured a nutty brownie, coconut macaroon, jelly donut, or another pastry. But not everyone shared Dennis' views.

"They're just doing their job, like you do your job," Marvin said, writing the mortgage check.

Dennis crossed his arms and leaned back on the side chair. "Do you ever think about Gerald, Dad? He wouldn't want this happening. He wouldn't want kids being manipulated, Dad. You know that."

"I think about your brother every day." Marvin closed the drawer and reached for his coffee mug. "There's nothing we can do about any of it."

A high school senior, class treasurer, believer of honesty and world peace, Dennis decided to do something about the situation. Familiar with campaigning and the perils of war, he made it his duty to try to save friends and associates.

"Listen, Rocco, I just heard you tell that guy you want to make your family proud." Dennis leaped over the counter. "You don't have to join the Marines. You need to go to college, get that degree you want, and marry Caroline, like you always talked about."

"But he said my mom will be proud of me, Dennis, and I know she will." Avoiding unyielding eyes, Rocco rolled an empty Captain Kid Cola can, moving it across spilled sugar. "No one ever joined the service in our family. They're all blue-collar men."

"What!" Dennis slapped Rocco's arm. "And the service isn't a blue-collar job?"

Lance Corporal Teahan had informed Rocco he could work his way up the ranks. "Earn more money, help your family, and have a good life," he said. "The Marines need good men like you."

"I'm going to college," Rocco avowed. "I'm looking into schools."

"We offer educational plans," the corporal assured. "You don't have to stay in the service forever. You can apply for a college plan."

Dennis had witnessed the entire scene. Sliding a tray of warm crullers onto the counter, he watched the Marine slink in to the café, approach Rocco, and sit next to him.

"And your relatives are alive, aren't they, Rocco?"

Nodding, Rocco grinned, a clownish grin, a fool's grin.

The first Marine from Abington, a homey, Massachusetts town, Rocco Marinoli boarded a Greyhound for boot camp, in North Carolina. Six hundred and eighty-four days later, proudly wearing uniforms trimmed with stripes and gold buttons, a sergeant and corporal drove Private Marinoli home, embalmed. Three cheers for the red, white and blue.

"Don't do it, Scotty!" Dennis pleaded. "We all love you. You're the king of the prom, the best looking guy in school!"

"I want to go," Scott Bridges mumbled, wiping chocolate from his mouth. "Besides, JT's over there."

"What?" Wanting to grind Scotty for meatloaf, Dennis pinched his friend. "You're saying because JT's there, you should be there?" Dennis pinched Scotty again, not hard enough as far as Dennis was concerned.

Rolling his neck, Scotty dully stated, "It doesn't seem fair I'm here and those guys are there."

"Life isn't fair, Scotty. You know that," Dennis said, poking his friend's chest, "and I know that. Sometimes life sucks, okay? But you've got a lot going for you."

"I got to go, Dennis. My father says it's the right thing to do," Scotty said, throwing a balled napkin across the room.

"That's not like you, littering. What's eating you?"

"Nothing seems the same. It hasn't in a few years. It's like nothing's inside me."

Thirteen months later, Scotty returned with something outside him. A plastic limb. Odd, though, his family had to chip in and buy him a leg that fit. You tell Scotty why.

"Help me out, Arnold," Dennis dragged Zack onto the Rochesters' back porch. "Convince him to stay here."

"Hell, no, don't stay here. Go to Canada, man," Arnold said, rolling a joint. "You can get some good stuff up there."

"I can't go to Canada," Zack responded, crushing a cola can. "My parents would murder me."

"Yah, but some yellow man can kill you, too, so where's the logic?" Arnold lit the joint, offered it, and quickly retracted, "Sorry. I forgot you guys don't smoke. Shit." He watched his refillable, brass lighter fall between floorboards.

"I'll never do drugs, mud for brains," Zack said, then laughed. "I don't need to get messed up."

"Then stopping drinking all that Captain Kid shit. What d'ya drink, six cans a day?"

Zack admitted to drinking at least four cans a day.

"Maybe you should use it in your gas tank," Arnold joked, reaching between the floorboards. "It'll get you and your car out of sight fast. Hell, don't hi-test your head. Use the shit to blast on up to Canada."

Zack never made it to Canada or boot camp. After deciding to tone up before shipping out, he jogged nine miles and dropped. A spry paperboy pedaling his Stingray bike through the park spotted Zack clutching his chest. By 1989, Zack had undergone two heart operations.

"What do you mean 'thinking about joining the army'! Are you out of your mind?" Dennis yanked Robin by his belt. "I heard what that guy said, but they're promises and lies! All of it!"

"L-l-let me g-g-go," Robin said, shoving Dennis. Confused about life, war, and love, he wanted to be anywhere than the café.

"That chocolate malt must have gone to your head, because that's the first I heard about your plan," Dennis lectured, shadowing Scotty up the street. "What about Lisa?"

"I'm j-j-joining the army, no m-m-matter what anyone says." Tugging a pack of Old Gold from his hip pocket, Robin walked faster, insisting he had made up his mind.

Three days later, after spending the better part of the week in bed, eating chocolate cookies, drinking Captain Kid Cola, morbidly celebrating Lisa's breakup with him, Robin changed his mind. Torn between unreciprocated love and hypocritical patriotism, he crawled from bed and drank twenty ounces of cola. With pins and needles sparking his legs like fireworks, he retrieved a few items from the garage, hiked a mature pine, slung a rope over a branch, and slipped his head into the loop. No need for Robin to change his physically ill mind again.

"My mother's getting married," Dylan Austin said, handing Dennis a dollar. "The guy just told me I'd be warm, safe, maybe even happy." Dylan wanted out of his mother's house.

There's nothing safe about Vietnam, Dennis thought, puzzled. "Did he actually use that word, 'safe'?"

"I think so." Dylan pressed Scotch-Tape on a box of donuts. "He promised me a few things."

"Promise yourself some things, Dylan. Promise to rent an apartment and get away from your mother's alcoholic boyfriend."

"It's bad." Dylan slid onto a chair. "Everything's out of control, and sometimes my head feels like it's going to bust."

"Then you shouldn't go, buddy." Slipping a straw into Dylan's cola can, Dennis encouraged him to stay in town and "see a doctor."

"I'll see someone. The recruiter promised me free medical care." Up and down, Dylan moved the straw.

Dylan moved a needle, too, in and out of his flesh. A year and a half after enlisting in the army, twenty-one-year-old Dylan Austin flew World Airlines, waited for his duffle bag, and slunk into an American evening, a full-blown heroin addict.

Agitated, Dylan rotated his thumbs. "Why'd you drive all the way to come here?" he asked. "Just because you think you know everything, Leighton?"

"I came because we're friends," Dennis said.

"It's no place for you, you with your silk house, goody two-shoe parents and freezer full of steak," Dylan stated, coldly. "I need more coffee." Standing, he lost balance and grabbed the table edge.

"Sit down, Dylan. I'll get you coffee."

In the cafeteria line, Dennis studied servicemen. Mostly young, they joked with one another, poured coffee, and swore. Two men, each holding a tray, ignored the other men.

An emerald in a mound of salt, a slight man shivered in the warm room. Not wanting to stare, Dennis looked away, but couldn't turn his mind from the scarecrow. Handing Dylan a hot cup, Dennis watched the scraggly fellow saunter toward the door. Twenty feet from their table, the man smiled, nervously. Dylan returned the cordiality. "Some men smoke out there. Some guys smoke in, some smoke out. In or out, it's a matter of choice," Dylan explained.

"Oh, that's cool," Dennis said, knowing not one thing about the hospital was hip.

Seventy-two miles from Abington, the veterans' hospital consisted of one emergency room, an x-ray department, a laboratory, thirty-four patient rooms, each containing a toilet, sink and four unappealing beds, an administrative office wing, a cafeteria, a lounge painted tan and an indoor basketball court—for who or what, Dennis didn't know. For sure, Dylan wasn't up to dancing the ball court.

Though physically intact, Dylan had arrived at the hospital a mental case. Paranoid and delusional, his mental status having changed under the influence of cola, coffee, frontline battle and heroin, marked from wrists to elbows, arms scarred from needles, Dylan spewed his insides into a chipped white metal bucket, with three roommates looking on.

According to every dusty, century-old dictionary, *warm*, *safe*, and *happy* did not apply to Dylan, but PFC Austin couldn't expect to receive private, first class treatment. According to higher-ups, Dylan should've been grateful to be alive.

"Rocco got lucky," Dylan said, and sighed. "Scotty's stuck with the shit forever."

"He's in college."

"Don't matter, Leighton. Don't you get it?" Dylan flicked Dennis' hand. "The stuff's in our minds. It's never going away."

Dennis wondered about the lifeless-looking straggler. Again, the fellow smiled. Dylan waved. "That poor bastard. Grew up in a family like yours, Leighton. Had it all, and then one day, a good eight years ago, trying not to pee his pants in the bush, someone offered him heroin, and it was all downhill from there. Been misplaced ever since."

Leaning on his father's desk, Dennis asked, "Where's Gerald buried?" Finding the question needless, Mr. Leighton ignored his son.

"Gerald?" Dennis stressed. "Where's he buried?"

Mr. Leighton fumbled for words. "He's in the soldiers' cemetery up north."

"Where 'up north'?" Dennis asked, unwrapping a piece of Bazooka Bubblegum. "Come on, Dad, don't try to con me."

Mr. Leighton clammed up. Not in the mood for his son's curiosity, he slapped Dennis on the back.

For nearly two years, Dennis had asked about Gerald. Missing his brother, trying to keep his memories fresh, Dennis pressed adults for answers. Marvin and Rose refused to talk about Gerald. Dennis' grandparents also shunned his questions. They remained silent or changed the subject. No wonder he finally stopped asking. Adults had conditioned Dennis to talk about subjects they deemed permissible.

Dennis pressured, "How did he die?"

"Come on, sport. You don't want to know."

"Yes, I do, Dad. We haven't talked about Gerald in six years."

"Maybe tomorrow, son. I have work to do."

Eyeing the scrappy serviceman, Dennis slid two jelly donuts from the bag. "How old is he, Dylan?"

Dylan pointed to a wheelchair-confined man. "Who him?"

"Not him," Dennis stated, annoyed. "The guy who goes out to smoke. The one who smiles?"

"That's Jimmy, an army guy. Maybe twenty-eight, at the most."

Dennis sneezed, a giant sneeze, nearly bowling Dylan over. Worried about getting sick, Dylan said he couldn't afford germs.

"I have allergies, bozo," Dennis said, and with another sneeze approaching, he cupped his face. He sneezed four times, loud.

"Hay fever." From behind, the scarecrow tugged Dennis' chair. "My kid brother had fits like those. Stand up and pinch your nose."

Believing he was going to faint, Dennis took a deep breath. He asked Jimmy to repeat what he said.

"Your nose," Jimmy said, noting the mole on Dennis' forehead. "Stand up and pinch it."

"It's you, Gerald," Dennis bluntly said, his knees knocking. "Is it you, Gerald?" He wanted to grab him, hug him, jump on him and wrap his legs around him, like when they were kids, but he held back, not sure who he was talking to.

Gerald James Leighton wept. "Denny?" he asked. "Is it really you?"

"Why'd you do it, Mom? Dad?" Enraged, Dennis ran up the hall stairs to retrieve his record player. On the platform, he turned. "Why? He's our flesh and blood!"

At a loss for long explanations, Mrs. Leighton said heroin destroys.

Marvin threw his pen at the wall. "The drugs! The craziness! The neighbors! Son," he said, "what did you expect us to do?"

Shaking the banister, Dennis exploded, "You could've told me the truth! You picked him up at the airport, told him to use his middle name, abandoned him, and told me he was dead! Gerald's my brother! He's my brother!"

"It's okay, Denny," Gerald said, lifting a tarp. "Mom and Dad didn't know what to do. I guess they worried about what the neighbors might say. Dad's a respected citizen of this town, and he. It's okay, Denny. Everything will be okay. You'll see."

Nothing special, with calendars taped to the walls, and the outside needing paint, the house welcomed three young men. They painted the outside white. Ten months later, every other day or so, a counselor wearing dungarees and holding a cigarette lighter left My Friends and I and welcomed a young man stepping from a car. Escorted by the counselor, each young man entered My Friends and I and signed himself in. Each recovering veteran believed in the promise of a brighter tomorrow.

18
Flipside

Photographer, Mike Dijital

Thank goodness, my nephew got me out. Why, if Jamie hadn't rescued me, I may still be jailed in the place. I spent two days there, and I can tell you there isn't a thing fancy or comfortable about the hospital. With nurses coming and going, and seeming like they're going, arriving frazzled and out of sorts, the cries in the night, and tit for tat arguments, it was sheer torture. For certain, there's no place like home. That's especially true when you're home and sane. Most people aren't. Most people think they're stable because they can't remember what stability is. Thank goodness, Jamie helped me remember my good days.

I drop to my knees every day, thanking Him for returning my peace of mind and intellect. Because if I listened to everyone else, including Dr. doesn't know paper towels from coffee filters, Elroy Jones, I would likely be swallowing pills for elderly dementia, drinking coffee, and bathing in the backyard nude. That's precisely what I meant: sunbathing in my birthday suit.

My neighbor assumed I was off my rocker, but Peggy envied my education, my Steinway, and my good cooking, so it's no surprise she disliked watching me hang sheets in the buff. Oh, we all know it's inappropriate to hang laundry naked in the yard. Of course, if you live on several acres, are surrounded by trees, separated from the rest of the world, and currently I am, you can do as you darn well please.

It's not from embarrassment that I moved. I moved to play my piano as loud as I want and mow my lawn whenever I choose without worrying about Peggy or anyone else calling the police. And if I decide to flap my nakedness in the wind, shaking wet socks, so be it. My life is mine. Thank goodness, I took it back.

After Peggy called the station, a policeman arrived at my house while I was dragging the empty basket across the lawn. "Are you okay, Miss Clark?" the fellow asked.

"Just fine, thanks," I slurred, waiting for the man in blue to open my back door. Thinking I was drunk, he wrapped his jacket around me, cuffed me, and escorted me to the police car.

At the station, the gent introduced me to a paramedic who gave me a tranquilizer and glass of Captain Kid Cola to wash it down, as if that would miraculously cure what ailed me. Small wonder 25% of the world's population is mentally ill. There isn't enough common sense to go around, but there's plenty of cola.

Standing next to me in the ER, Dr. Jones asked Rachel if mental illness ran in the family. "I don't think so," my niece responded. Gawking at me, she knew I wouldn't help her answer. Twisting my long, white hair—burnt sienna, straight from a bottle, for the outside world—into knots, I had retreated deep into myself, a familiar place I went when annoyed, because I don't like hospitals, and I detest doctors, especially poking and prodding where they don't have business being. Know-it-all nurses who don't know much don't belong around me either.

"To tell you the truth, my aunt Paula is a bit odd," Rachel alleged, huddled with the doctor.

My sister is not odd. Two years my senior, Paula is brilliant. When she was twenty, she filled a backpack with everyday essentials, jumped into Richard Turner's convertible, and drove from Rhode Island to San Francisco, where they connected with Oakley Lewis, Richard's boyfriend. He put them up in his four-room apartment on Delores Street for a year, rent-free. Odd? You decide.

Dr. Jones didn't care about Paula, and he certainly didn't give a hoot about my health, because he diagnosed me with Alzheimer's dementia and admitted me to a ward on the third floor. Then he went golfing.

"That's right," a slender nurse informed Jamie, "Dr. Jones 'is golfing' this afternoon."

"You better call someone," my adorable prince said, "because I'm taking my aunt home."

"You can't. She has a fever, high white blood cell count and high sedimentation rate." Looking at me funny—as though my health interfered with her free time—the nurse must've thought I was deaf, too. She strongly added, "Besides, only Rachel Wood can sign her out."

Jamie wouldn't accept that. One step ahead of white sneaker wearers, he boldly questioned, "Can you tell me what an elevated sedimentation rate means?"

"Generally it means infection. That something's wrong with the immune system," the nurse said, and smiled, maybe thinking my nephew was single. She went on to say, "In many cases, it means dementia. That's normal with elderly patients."

At the time, I was sixty-eight, young enough to be ill and know it, and old enough to be crazy and not know. But as far as the nurse was concerned, I couldn't be both. Ill or crazy. Heads or tails?

Jamie called her, but Rachel wasn't home. At Pine Hill nursing home, my niece busily inspected rooms, spoke with nurses, and reviewed costs. She didn't know what to look for, and evidently neither did Dr. Jones, because I wasn't crazy, not in the sense doctors use the word—like a child tossing a beach ball. Suffering brain poisoning from daily caffeine, I was ill, and I was crazy as a result of the illness. Not one health care worker figured that out. No wonder psychiatrists make out like bandits.

God bless my nephew, and I'll say it over and over. God bless Jamie, because he knew something was wrong after I asked for the afternoon *Listener*.

"Aunt Celestine, that paper stopped printing five years ago."

That's approximately how long I was ill. After I left the school, for about five years, my focus progressively dwindled, my intellect deteriorated and poor judgment let loose.

"Have you been painting again, Aunt Celestine?" Jamie asked. Brushing my hair, he reminded me of the fumes.

Turpentine and oils go to my head and fog me, but I'm no Rembrandt, and I know when to put the easel away.

"No," I remarked, rather snippy, "and I could use a cup of tea."

When Jamie reminded me that I don't drink tea, I noticed the fear in his face. The poor kid thought I had lost my mind without reason.

God in Heaven, pray for our sinners, including doctors and nurses, because they are damning people into sinning and sentencing them to hell. They're working for the devil.

Slapping the brush from Jamie's hand, I said I would drink whatever I wanted. Lowering his head, my nephew left my bedside to get me tea.

I shoved the cup across my tray, spilling the hot liquid. "What's wrong?" Jamie asked, wiping the little puddle with a tissue. "You asked for tea."

With my hand hurting from the IV needle, and my head clearing from the IV fluid, in between tears, I said, "I only drink coffee."

I wasn't sobering up from ingesting alcohol. The smell alone annoys me. I was coming back from a five-year caffeine toot.

I didn't have elderly dementia. Does anyone, really? I was purely "schizophrenic." The mental changes were brought about by changes in my body's chemistry, brought about by coffee and chocolate desserts. Poison seeped from my bloodstream into my head. I know you don't need a visual, not before lunch, but it's the only way I can describe it.

Dr. Jones believed I was too old to develop schizophrenia. My good Lord, the world is not flat. What did they teach him in medical school? How to match his shoes with his tie? Schizophrenia does not exist, and from medical ignorance, temporarily I forfeited my mental existence.

It's embarrassing enough that I hung laundry in the nude, but I socialized with Norman Daniels, and the day after I joined Norman in the sleigh the women in Millie's Hair Salon talked. So a little hay stuck to my head. The hayride was public; eleven cheerful holidayers celebrated with us in that hay. I've seen dust, lint and other artifacts on women's clothes. In fact, one morning I took Georgia aside and mentioned the grape gum on her bottom. No shame in that. And surely there's no sin in riding the streets in a truck full of hay with a gray-haired fellow old enough to be my father. I never slept with Norman. I needed to talk. That was all, a friendship based on conversation. I can't recall most of what I said. My mind whirled too fast to process normally. That's why Peggy caught glimpse of naked me in my backyard.

After morning coffee and my shower, wanting to be on time for my eye doctor appointment, I searched for my sweater, the one with navy blue buttons. Unable to locate it, I assumed it might be on the line. Near the door, I grabbed the full laundry basket, and without considering my nakedness, rushed outside and hung laundry. By the time the towels were hung, I realized I was in my naked truth. The damage was done. I hung the sheets.

It disturbed me the policeman called my niece, because I don't want anyone bothering Rachel with my problems. Sheltered most her life, she's a sweet lady, married with twins, but a lady without guts can't free a hostage from the hospital.

After a nurse asked if I needed anything, I asked for my nephew. He's the one with spunk.

A few years ago, Jamie lived in an eight-room house with Danny, a barber with hair to his hips, and Mark Bumpus, the drummer for Hell and High Water, a local group, from Providence. Littered with newspapers, empty drinking glasses and wooden pipes, the house wasn't anything special. I often stopped by and offered to clean, but my nephew told me not to worry about the mess. Once Jamie actually said, "We read and whittle, Auntie. I'll make sure to carve you a few pipes for Christmas."

The place stunk. I assumed the odor was weed, you know, pot, but Jamie assured me the smell was incense. Come to find out, my instinct was on target. Mixed with the smell of sweet cocaine, a poor man's lover, marijuana odor lingered. I shouldn't say which roommate used what, since Mark's father is a well-known man, but they were all guilty.

Two policemen cuffed the three of them after a neighbor complained about them climbing the roof. They fled from people, invisible intruders. One of the fathers called in a favor, and the boys were released without charges after they agreed to sign themselves into a rehabilitation facility.

"Jamie," I had said, smoothing his cheek with the back of my hand, "you don't use drugs."

Heartbroken, lost in the land of adrenaline-induced denial, I didn't want to hear the truth, but Gilda Bumpus gave it to me straight. "Celestine," she said, breaking a wooden pipe, "wake up! Did you actually think they whittled these for Christmas presents?"

Christmas had come and gone, and without the pipes my nephew promised. I had to face reality. "Try to relax, Gilda. I understand Jamie was tinkering with drugs."

"'Tinkering'? The boys were not tinkering!" Gilda screamed. "They are full-blown cocaine addicts and just got out of the worst jam of their lives!" Gilda threw a corkscrew into Mark's suitcase.

My nephew kissed me on the cheek. "I'll go to Donut World and grab a coffee."

Examining the European blonde in the next bed, I worried about bed bugs. Scratching her arms, the stranger picked little scabs, and without bothering to wash her hands, she took a few Choco-Bites from her candy bowl and offered them to me. I wasn't hungry.

Delighted to see Jamie with a cup of coffee, I smiled. "Just a touch of cream," my nephew stated. "The way you like it."

After swallowing the first sips of warm poison, I shook like a catfish pulled from the stream. Jamie mentioned my unsteady state. Then he asked when I started ingesting coffee.

"About thirty years ago," I replied, "but I started drinking more coffee, five years ago, at the beauty parlor."

My nephew pulled the cup away. "I think it's the culprit," he said. "I know caffeine acts like cocaine. You're high, Aunt Celestine. It all makes sense. You're acting like I did when I was cranked on cocaine!"

"Don't be ridiculous! Coffee doesn't harm anyone! Besides, I would never get high." I wanted to finish the gloomy drink.

Used to the misery source, used to loss of focus and intellectual depreciation, I believed I would've been lost without coffee. On the contrary, I was lost with it. Not knowing it, I was higher than a red balloon floating across the Mojave Desert.

A nurse was about to inject my roommate when Jamie asked her to test my blood again. "There's no need," she said. "Abnormal lab results go with the territory."

Jamie smiled. "And I breakfast with a lawyer every week."

"I'll call Dr. Jones," the nurse said.

Several months after I removed caffeine from my diet, my blood returned to normal. My brain cleared, and I recovered completely. Soon after healing, I traded Connecticut and the robins for Maine, where I play my piano and listen to the chickadees sing. I don't plan on hanging laundry in the nude. That isn't normal for me, retired from teaching at St. Edward's Elementary. However, I may learn to square dance and play the harp, dress-required activities.

19
Can't Blame it on the Cow

Photo by Michael Connors

Ricky may have told you something else, but we were there. Thirteen at the time, we took part in the whole thing.

The menu hung on the cafeteria wall. Pizza or cheese macaroni, green beans or corn, a brownie or lemon sherbet. Most classmates selected pizza, corn and the brownie and bought Captain Kid Cola. We all received a half-pint milk, part of the nutritional plan, but no one except a few girls and Wilbur Parkinson drank milk, because half the time it was sour. We were, too, a group of eighteen, in seventh grade.

It shouldn't have happened, but that's how it goes when hyperactive kids get together and gang up on someone. In our class, that someone was Wilbur.

May 1981, Wilbur seemed like an odd kid. A bringer, that's what Ricky and I called the kids who brought lunch, a bit pudgy in the cheeks with an oval face, brown hair and skinny limbs, Wilbur sat in the last seat of the last row, keeping to himself. Sometimes he showed up at school looking as if he'd slept in his trousers and shirt, but he kept good grades, and he had a paper route, delivering to over forty customers a day.

Wilbur didn't skate, and he never joined Little League or Boy Scouts, so I never knew what he was really about. After it happened, I learned his father had a heart problem, and his mother died when he was young. The oldest of four children, Wilbur delivered papers to help buy groceries.

On the day it happened I left for the skating rink before breakfast. A Pow-Wow hockey skater, I drank twelve ounces of Black Lightning Cola in the bleachers. Afterward, I devoured a bowl of Krackly Kokos. I arrived at school hyper, but couldn't tell you then. Thirteen years old, I didn't know what hyperactive meant.

During second period, history, Deidre, my girlfriend at the time, handed me a box of chocolate-covered raisins. I shouldn't have eaten in class, but we sat at the back, and I was bored. I ate the raisins and took my restlessness out on Wilbur. "Psst, Parkinson," I whispered, loud enough for Ricky and a few others to hear. "Why yesterday's clothes? Your momma can't do laundry?" A few classmates laughed, but it wasn't funny. Unable to sit still, I entertained myself picking on Wilbur.

When lunch rolled around, irritable and hungry, I bought pizza, corn and the brownie. After eating, I was still hungry, because they never gave anyone enough. Deidre offered me her brownie. I asked if she was sure, pulling the thing from her hand.

After eating the second brownie, I felt like King Kong. Believing myself invincible, I started in on Wilbur. "Drink your milk, cowboy," I ordered.

Laughing, Ricky crunched his cola can. Then, quickly composing himself—if you can call what happened next composed—he strolled to Wilbur's table and shoved his milk carton at the kid. "Drink it, or I'll make you."

Avoiding adding to the scene, Wilbur drank Ricky's half-pint. Then I handed Wilbur my milk. Leaning over him, I insisted he drink it. "I'm full," he said politely, but I threatened him with a fist. Wilbur drank.

Douglas and Peters lined up, forcing Wilbur to drink their half-pints. Ricky and I cheered. Deidre ordered us to stop, but I couldn't. Something inside me let loose, and though I recalled my parents teaching me about being nice to others and treating everyone as I would want them treating me, heartless, I urged, "Chug! Chug!"

I laughed ruthlessly, watching the poor kid drink milk, seven in all. Afterward, he fled to the bathroom. I never saw him again.

Mr. Parkinson underwent heart surgery two weeks before the incident and was recuperating when the school nurse called him. He grabbed his keys, rushed to his van, and drove to the school.

On their way home, he slowed at the corner of Oak and Grove Streets, before the intersection. The station wagon behind them never did. Going 60 MPH it slammed the van. Reaching to save his son, Mr. Parkinson suffered a heart attack. Flying through the windshield, Wilbur broke his neck.

Wilbur never should have died, but maybe we all have a deadline. Thirty years old, I'm diabetic. I developed diabetes sometime during my senior summer, working at the coffee bean factory. Picking out runts, I stood in line eight hours, smelling coffee.

My doctor warned me to stay away from sugar, chemicals, and all artificial ingredients. The changed diet calmed me, and probably added years to my life. I wish Wilbur could know me now, and Ricky, too.

When it happened, Ricky was twenty-one and on medication, prescribed speed for ADD. He was a good guy and didn't have any major problems, but the ADD diagnosis bothered him, and the medicine seemed to backfire, like it put him in another world.

One afternoon, while we ate chocolate cookies in my kitchen, Ricky told me he felt stigmatized.

"Don't worry," I said. "Lots of kids are taking drugs for ADD."

Ricky and I sat there, talking about ADD, why it affected him, and why so many kids are taking stimulants for loss of focus and hyperactivity. After it happened, I learned stimulants cause loss of focus and hyperactivity, and that contrary to what doctors may think, prescribed stimulants don't cure hyperactivity. They dull a child's judgment and intellect. The drugs poison the brain, taking away the real person behind the mask.

Sometimes I blame myself. I probably should have been around more for Ricky. Worried about my sick grandmother, I read her books and helped clean her house. Maybe I should've been with my friend, but my parents insist I'm not responsible for the world.

He took the pipe. Ricky closed his father's garage and stuck the thing in his mouth. His mother found him, blue, his head back, stiff.

Not one person, not even me, noticed Ricky slipping away. My friend must've been in a deep stupor, a tennis ball stuck in mud, to kill himself. How can clear-headed people commit suicide? I don't think they can. Life has something for everyone.

Ricky's little sister, April, attends college. "I think I understand why my brother committed suicide," she said. "It must have been his diet. He drank so much cola. It was like he lived on it. I don't know what to do about it, but Ricky would want me to do something, to help other children."

April and I ping-ponged it for a time, discussing how caffeine causes hyperactivity. We also believe caffeine causes people to lose control, torment others, become violent, and commit suicide. After all, children used to be a little restless, but now they're psychotic. They're a spoonful over the line on something. Caffeine.

20
Sunny Daze

Dedicated to Butch and Dixie

Olive Chambers knew her visit would end soon. To the right of the brick building, behind pines and birches, the sun lowered itself. The sunset always spoiled their time together.

"Have some frappe," Olive said, edging the paper cup across the night table. "It's your favorite, Nell. Remember when we fell in love with these?"

Frail, Nell rubbed her hazel eyes. "I sure do."

Working for Raffael's clothing store, in 1951, Olive and Nell dressed mannequins. Mondays and Fridays, the young women spent their lunch break at Wimsie's, a sweet parlor. One afternoon, Mr. Farraday, the owner, whipped up a batch of chocolate frappe and asked the girls to sample it.

"Sal got a kick out of us sitting there, on the red spinning stools, our eyes wide, mouths watering. I'll never forget the first taste, Nell. It was heaven. Full of frappe, we had trouble dressing the doll. Remember we almost put her blouse on backward?"

Nell flatly responded, "We laughed and laughed." Restless, beneath the sheet, Nell's tense legs moved.

"We sure did. Boy, did we laugh. And soon after, Sal added chocolate frappe to the menu. Remember I stopped drinking chocolate frappe? I had to," Olive said. "I broke out in pimples in my twenties. I swore it was the chocolate, but I guess we'll never know. I switched to vanilla, and I never changed back."

"Those were the days." Nell wiped sticky fluid from her eyes. "May I have a tissue?"

"It's your eyes again, Nell, isn't it? How long have they bothered you this time?"

Reaching for the small box of Softwipes, Nell told her friend not to worry. "My eyes will be fine."

"You'll be okay, Nell. Stewart and I will make sure of it. You'll have the best care." Turning to the window, Olive silently bid the sun

97

farewell, as she watched a nurse water a potted plant.

"Jay will help me. You know how he likes to take care of me."

Nell's husband would've taken care of her, if he could have. Buried in St. Bernadette's Cemetery, Jay died seventeen years earlier.

"It's not schizophrenia, Mrs. Chambers. Nell is too old," Dr. Holiday explained, the first day the women visited him.

After checking Nell's blood pressure and pulse, unable to offer any salvation, Dr. Holiday invited Olive into the hall. "Alzheimer's takes its toll on family and friends, as well as its victim," Dr. Holiday claimed. "It is a dreadful disorder, Mrs. Chambers. Your friend will struggle with memory loss and focus until the day she dies."

Olive moved Nell's head slightly to the left. "What about her eyes, Dr. Holiday? Lately, she's been having problems with them. They seem to water for no reason."

Bending for a better look, Dr. Holiday stated, "Probably an allergy or two. People tend to pick them up as they age."

As she aged, Nell picked up additional frappe, acquired a taste for cappuccino, and never turned down Lorna's homemade fudge or chocolate chiffon cake at the Senior Center's get-togethers. And once, only once, Nell picked up a transient.

Briskly walking across the town common, searching for Pecan, her rambunctious cat that left the porch, Nell shouted, "Come here, kitty, kitty!" Tugging her red scarf closer, she almost tripped over a makeshift coverall hiding a young man. Squatting beneath a blanket under a barren oak, the bearded fellow shivered, smoking a Marlboro.

Taken aback, Nell ogled the vodka bottle, partially wrapped in newspaper on the ground beside him. "It's too cold for man and beast," Nell cautioned, her breath visible. Barely an adult, the forlorn stranger stared at the old woman.

"Where is your family, dear?" Nell asked, then shouted, "kitty, kitty!" Her focus shifted again. "Where do you live?" The young adult offered no answers.

For the night, Dirk resided at Nell's house. She poured him a bath, served chicken, baked potatoes and coffee, and read him articles from *The Daily Bean*.

"You what!" Leaning over her porch, Olive shook a dust mop. "It's too dangerous nowadays to be taking in strangers! What were you thinking?"

Nell had thought about the Noonan boy, Charles. "Dirk's sharp eyes resembled Charles' eyes. I guess I retreated in time."

During their second meeting, Dr. Holiday whispered, "Mrs. Chambers, your friend is delusional. There's not a chance Nell took in a stranger. She may not be all there, but she knows the difference between right and wrong." Normal volume, he asked, "Do you know the difference between right and wrong, Nell?"

Nell pulled cat hair from her pants. "Yes, I do."

"But her eyes, doctor." Olive worried about them.

"I'll give her a nasal decongestant. It might help."

The only thing Nasaway helped was Nell's bizarre state, pushing the elderly woman further into her gateway between truth and fantasy, trust and suspicion, and good and evil, and it increased her racing.

"Slow down!" Huffing, Olive trailed Nell up Park Avenue. "We have time to visit all the stores! It's only noon!"

Soon after the women's weekend break, Nell's daughter called Dr. Holiday. "I don't know how to take care of my mother," Patricia said. "She's phoning at all hours, asking me to take her to bring my father his lunch."

Believing it best, safe for Nell and easier on the family, Dr. Holiday suggested a nursing home. "Your mother will receive good care," the doctor stated.

The nurse drew the curtain, and without saying a word, she exited Nell's private room. Looking around for a wastebasket, Olive crunched the paper cup.

Nell said she might take in a movie. "Or watch *All in the Family*. Isn't that Archie something? Jay thinks so."

"It's getting late, sweetie," Olive said. She dreaded leaving but disliked the surreal more. "I'll ask the nurse to bring you a cup of tea."

"It's good to see you, Iris. Did Pug ask Jay to help with the bomb shelter?"

21
Top O' the Morning

Athens State Hospital, Circa 1907

An only child, Randy Newman cared for his aged mother. Nearly every morning he carefully draped his purple scarf, the one with little yellow elephants stamped throughout the silk, around Bea's white hair and tied it beneath her sagging chin. After propping his mother into her wheelchair, he rolled Bea onto the porch, to the back corner, where spreading rhododendrons shaded her. There, Bea waited for the mailman, a small pleasure she had always enjoyed.

"Good morning, Mrs. Newman," Eric Wallace, the nearsighted mailman said, one morning, like every morning he arrived, as Randy drank coffee on a wicker chair, petting his mother's hand.

"Lovely day," Randy said, and smiled.

Eric stuffed mail into the curbside box. "How's your mother feeling?"

Although the previous day Randy admitted Bea was under the weather, Randy claimed she felt fine. "Come on, Mom, wave to the mailman. It's rude to ignore him. He's here every day." Randy lifted his mother's hand and waved with her.

After Bea's monthly pension check arrived, Randy clasped his mother's hand and slipped the pen between taut fingers. Pressing her hand, he helped his mother sign her name. "No more worries about bills," Randy said, in a higher than normal voice.

Retired from South Light Company, the sixty-nine-year-old bachelor believed he was doing the right thing. Using Bea's money, Randy paid utilities and purchased groceries: chocolate bars, carrots, Captain Kid Cola, coffee, chocolate syrup, hamburger, cookies, salted crackers, typical food for a not so typical mother and son. Bea never complained.

"Cat's finally caught your tongue," Randy joked, one evening, pouring himself cappuccino, made with a new stainless steel cappuccino maker, the one he bought for Valentine's Day.

Without a lover or friends, Randy gifted himself. An iced tea maker and a Turkish coffeepot collected dust in the pantry. Bea never said a word, quite unlike her, especially since she threw a sponge at her son the afternoon he carried a used bicycle and beach umbrella into the house. "We didn't need them!" Bea yelled. "How old do you think you are?"

Stuck in his seventeenth year, Randy was elderly, and he knew it, but time stood still for Randy. Time and life.

"I'll be on vacation next week, Mr. Newman. A young fellow is taking over. How's your mother?" Eric shoved the mail into the box.

Randy swallowed coffee, then he lifted his mother's hand. "She's fine, Mr. Wallace, and you?"

"I'm well. Looking forward to a rest."

The weekend passed slowly, but Randy filled his time. He put all 1,000 cardboard pieces of Marilyn Monroe, his favorite actress, together.

Monday morning, Randy waited for the mailman. "He's late, Mom." Randy held his mother's hand. "Don't worry," he said. "He'll be here."

Lance Marble stared at the couple. "Are you Mr. Newman?"

Standing, Randy said he was Newman. As the mailman advanced, Randy instructed him to leave the mail in the box.

"You better bring your mother in," Lance advised, Wednesday morning. "The rain's right behind me."

Randy grabbed the chair handles. "Just leave it in the box."

"Top o' the morning," Officer Mick Donovan said, addressing Randy through the screen door. "I have your mother's mail. I'd like to speak with her. Your mother went to school with my father, Mr. Newman, and he's been dead for over eighteen years. I'd like to know her secret."

"My mother is sleeping," Randy said. He bit a fingernail.

"I'm sure she is, but I need to see her." Mick knew not to scream or cry about the situation. "You can let me in, and we'll discuss it quietly, Mr. Newman, or you can go down to the station in cuffs."

In the living room, Randy listened and wept. "...and Eric can't see well, but the other mailman, the new guy, sees very good," Mick explained. "He found it odd your mother never changed her scarf."

Mick carefully folded the wheelchair. "You better call someone, Randy. Let a relative or friend know you'll be at the state hospital. There's no guarantee they'll let you out for the services."

101

22
Me Too

Dedicated to a man and his boat

Like baking the winning apple pie for the County Fair Contest, healing is an art. If you make a medical error, a patient may win a ticket to the morgue. Similarly, if you lack the best technique or add the wrong ingredients, your pie loses the contest, you lose your pride, and the dumpy woman behind the pin curls walks away with the blue ribbon and gift certificate for a day at Home Spa.

Meghan Burke's cousin, a nurse, sort of, having the degree and training, rarely cooked. But if Frances placed her pie on the contest table, she would've gloated about its cracked crust and bubbled out apples, expecting to hear the judge call her name for first place. Never second. Goodness gracious, third was more than an insult.

Sometimes a person in the family thinks she's better than everyone else. In Meghan's family, that was Frances South. The registered nurse believed her personality and medical advice to be first rate, like Celia Casey's apple pie. But Frances helped kill her grandfather, decades later her cousin and, well, you can count the others on your fingers. Coffee-loving Frances didn't mean to shorten Grandpa Nelson's life. It just happened, after she opened her mouth. Sometimes that's how it goes in the world of caffeinated medical professionals.

Harry Nelson was an old fellow. Born at the turn of the century, he lived through World Wars I and II, a motorcycle accident, the Depression, President Kennedy's assassination, the Vietnam War, Grandma's fits of rye, a mugging in the park, a kidney loss, and pneumonia. By the time the doctor at the hospital diagnosed lung cancer, Grandpa had played with caffeine, whiskey, nicotine, cyclamate, MSG, and a handful of other poisons.

Though elderly, Harry was a survivor, and he loved life. Always following his doctor's advice, he believed he would live another ten years.

After Dr. Clemens ordered Harry to quit smoking, Harry put down his cigarettes. Nonsmokers might think that smart, because nicotine is a

102

chemical many accuse of causing cancer. However, any stimulant likely causes cancer. Try to keep it hush, hush, because people may get better if you spread the word.

Frances missed the opportunity to lecture about the dangers of nicotine. Perhaps the financially stable woman rehearsed a speech but forgot what to say when she stood at her grandfather's front door, asking for money to buy tires. That's how it was with several family members. They focused on what Harry could give them.

After he stopped smoking, Harry sucked on hard candy, peppermints and Root Beer Barrels, to keep his saliva flowing, and he crawled up the porch steps. After chemo treatments, a taxi delivered Harry to his house. He smiled at neighbors, inched the few feet to the porch steps, crouched, and with nausea and pain overwhelming, crawled up six steps leading to the front door. Behind him, Meghan offered her hands. Yankee pride catalyzed Harry's refusal. Determined, the brave soul made it across the deck.

We might like to believe Frances was concerned about Grandpa's best interest, that she contributed positively when it came to her grandfather's health, but she had one too many cups of coffee, two cups, the morning she interrupted Dr. Clemens discussing chemotherapy. "He's too old," Frances barked, twirling a spoon in her Grand Canyon mug. "No more chemo for Mr. Nelson."

You're correct. It wasn't Frances' job to make up Grandpa's mind, but you overlooked an important detail. Many medical workers are like beads snapped together as a necklace. The opinion of one doctor commonly links with the next, right or wrong. And after Frances, a caffeine addict and charge nurse at the hospital, lectured the physician on her grandfather's quality of life, the doctor conveniently agreed with her. He stopped Harry's chemo. The doctor didn't immediately discontinue treatments. After the third treatment, Clemens neglected to offer Harry additional treatments. Cancer spread to his bladder.

Creeping down the staircase, Harry complained about "dribbling in his pants." "I can't live like this," the gent mumbled, and he crept up the stairs to change.

"You'll be okay, Grandpa," Meghan assured.

"I know I will. They'll have to give me a bag or something. I hope they don't give me diazepam. I don't do well with that."

Meghan carried Grandpa's blue suitcase into a room at the hospital. "Would you like to stay for lunch?" her grandfather asked. Lunch, Meghan imagined, would be a dry tuna sandwich and half pint of milk.

She declined the offer but should've stayed, because after Grandpa left the hospital, Harry Nelson wasn't Grandpa at all. Under the care of medical professionals, Harry became poisoned from diazepam.

Documented in Mr. Nelson's medical folder for ten years, the man was allergic to diazepam, critical information. And yet, not one health care professional knew this. Either the medical team neglected to read Mr. Nelson's file because he was elderly, or because Frances gave the order to let Mr. Nelson die, or because they were plain lazy, or because coffee stripped their ability to follow through with daily routines. Regardless of the reason, Dr. Clemens ordered diazepam, a nurse delivered it, and without anyone telling the man what the little pill was Grandpa Nelson swallowed it.

Experiencing severe allergic response, Harry lost his mind as his compromised body filled up with fluid. Nurses called the dignified man psychotic.

Meghan would've spent her life savings to spend a normal day with her grandfather, but Harry never recovered from cancer, the allergic reaction, or caffeine's effects. Three weeks after leaving the hospital, with Meghan at his side, Grandpa Nelson died in his brass bed. In his living room, Frances chewed a chocolate softie, dusting golden teacups from Occupied Japan.

23
Eleventh Grade Chemistry

Photo by Troy Newell

I'm disappointed teachers don't teach students how caffeine affects the brain. A half-hour lesson would've spared my mother and me from our harrowed experiences.

It happened to me during my junior year. Sitting in Mr. Moran's class, reading *Catcher in the Rye*, I couldn't focus.

"Then what did the protagonist do, Miss Wheeler?" Mr. Moran asked. Lost mentally, I didn't know.

"May I be excused to see the nurse?"

"Aren't you feeling well, Miss Wheeler?"

Mr. Moran was concerned, and so was I, because I never lost focus before. She did though. My mother lost focus, organizational skills and more. At thirty-nine years old, my mother lost her mind.

Throwing things, spoons, coffee cups, books, anything she got her hands on, my mother vented at my father, my brother, and me. "I can't take it!" she screamed, as if someone had broken her arm.

My father asked, "Honey, do you need to talk about something?"

At that time, "No!" was all she said.

Six months later, she sat with a psychiatrist. Not a believer of outside therapy, my mother really didn't want to. She preferred reading books, trying to find out what was wrong with her.

"A mineral deficiency?" my mother mumbled, one afternoon, sitting on the camelback sofa, reading *Everything You Need to Know to Balance Your Body*. She dropped another sugar cube into her coffee. Soon after drinking the coffee, she screamed about how we didn't appreciate her.

Dr. Lipschultz, the psychiatrist, appreciated her, a sandy blonde with a tight face, almost like a mask, but evidently he didn't hear what she explained. He gave my mother lithium, which temporarily deadened her to the outside world, allowing her to cope. The strange thing is that my mother didn't have much to cope with. Sure, she cleaned and cooked as much as she wanted, but my father never expected a lilywhite home or six-course meal every evening. He loved my mother for the tranquil woman he fell in love with.

"Kiss my ass, Jason!" she screamed. My father wanted to dine out, but my mother insisted, "I worked on this lasagna all day! You'll all sit down and eat it!"

I stopped bringing friends home because my mother embarrassed me. How would you like your mother telling your best friend she needs to lose weight? Or have your mom slink around the house in a short nightgown?

I felt like a mistreated dog, left to lap the morsels of affection long after they had been devoured by someone else. I was lost without my mother's attention.

Face to face with my mother, I wanted to run. Never knowing what was going to come out of her mouth, I braced myself for the worse, gritting my teeth.

Many times I was with her, and on occasions I wasn't, such as in school, I shook. An emotional wreck, not knowing about biochemistry at the time, I never had time to calm down. A seventh grader, I concentrated on getting through the day, hoping the yelling would stop.

My mother's mood swings never completely ended back then, even after she took a selective serotonin reuptake inhibitor, a SSRI, a drug that works like prozac, to balance her moods. The psychiatrist prescribed it. He said lithium wasn't "getting the job done."

My mother wasn't getting the job done as a homemaker and wife. Magazines on the rug didn't bother my father, but cucumber and carrot peels dirtying the sink did, and the chicken. My mother left a chicken in the sink for three days. It thawed and smelled.

"What's going on, Elizabeth?" my father asked, scraping dried carrot from the sink, after returning from a meeting in Margate, New Jersey. "We don't live like this."

Many times I thought about asking my mother what was wrong. Traumatized from her moods, I figured she'd chop my face off, like after I asked about the toothpaste in the sink.

A toothpaste chunk and spittle in the bathroom disturbed me. I would have cleaned it, but my mother may have yelled, and I knew if I didn't clean it she might yell. In a no-win situation, I approached my mother as she ground Afternoon Delight coffee beans. "Mom, don't you wash the sink anymore?"

"You're old enough to pitch in around here, Catherine! Your father's out of town more than he's here, and who do you think helps me? No one! I handle the day-to-day crap by myself! If you have a problem with the sink, clean it, you brat!"

I wondered how she would react to what I was thinking about saying, but I said it anyhow—"Did you take your medication?" Slap! My mother's hand hit my face so fast and furiously that I fell against the table. Hiding my face with my hands, I said I was sorry, over and over. She didn't apologize. My mother called me all sorts of filthy names, names I never heard in school.

The beginning of the end arrived after my mother decided to go back to college. "To be a nurse. I'll make a great nurse," she said, buttering my father's wheat toast.

"Whatever you want, honey," my father said, and smiled. "Whatever makes your mother happy, Catherine and Robby, makes me happy."

For about two months, my mother complained and yelled nonstop, but my father, brother and I played basketball in the driveway, and we rode our bicycles, dodging her moods. With the fall weather, everyone seemed happy, but we hid our emotions, trying not to upset one another. Then it hit.

"I'm moving into a dorm."

"You're what?" Clearly upset, my father scrunched his eyebrows. "Say it again, Elizabeth."

"The dorm. I'll study better there."

We sat there, at Carmello's Restaurant, eating our swordfish, I suppose because my father, a grape juice and water drinker, rarely yells. The after show was horrid, though, and there's no need for me to get into it, except to say my mother moved that weekend, into a dorm.

She never graduated. My mother attended college for several months, until Christmas break, but by then she wasn't retaining anything.

"Come home," my father said. "I'll get you help. You need help."

"I don't need help, Jason." She spoke funny, as if bricks weighed her tongue down. "I'm getting an apartment to work through some things. I need to be on my own for a bit, away from you."

"No, Elizabeth." He dragged her laundry bag to the door. "You're not. You can forget about me, but you have a son and daughter that need you."

Leaning against a bookcase in the dirty dorm room, not knowing what to say, I asked my mother to come home. I added, "I love you."

"No, you don't. You're a big girl, daddy's girl."

I wanted to hug her, throw my arms around her, but my mother scared me. "I do love you," I said.

"I love you, too," Robby said, timidly.

"Don't mock me! Jason, can't you teach them anything!"

Running to the door, my mother said she needed coffee. "Because you three do a number on my head!"

New Year's came and went, again. My birthday came and went, again. We hadn't heard anything from her for two years when my father decided to move.

"We can't leave this town," I argued. "I have friends here. Please, Dad, don't make us move."

"This town is going down, Catherine, with drug dealers and homeless people. It's better for all of us if we move."

"What about Mom? What if she comes home?"

"Catherine, your mother wants to stay away. It's her choice," my father said.

We moved a few towns away, close to Pennsylvania. At least once a month, I returned to New Jersey to visit Erin, my best friend.

Roller-skating past Casino Blue, I spotted a woman on a doorstep, drinking cola. Appalled by her condition, a torn pink sweater clinging to her wasted frame, dirty hair and sunken cheeks, I decided not to point her out to Erin. Skating on, I didn't want to upset my friend, but I knew I had seen my mother.

I've never been ashamed of my mother because I've always loved her. I don't blame her for what happened. I blame the psychiatrist for giving my mother pills instead of treating the real problem. I blame food agencies, researchers, and doctors. I blame our higher-ups for not knowing what they're doing when it comes to the public's health and safety.

Leaving Mr. Moran's room, I knew what to say and what not to say. If I told Mrs. Geary the truth, she wouldn't believe me. If I lied, I would be lying for the right reasons.

"My leg hurts."

Mrs. Geary shoved a thermometer into my mouth. "Did you bang your leg?" she asked.

"Yes. On a chair."

"Is the pain sharp or dull?"

"Dull."

"You'll be fine," Mrs. Geary said, handing me an aspirin.

"No, thanks. I don't like pills."

"Aspirin is harmless. You can buy it over the counter. Take it."

"Thanks anyway, but I hurt and want to go home."

Behind the wheel of Daddy's Cadillac, the beautiful woman with flawless skin handed me a can of lemonade. "How are you feeling, dear?" she asked. Grabbing her tightly, I hugged my tranquil mother.

You bet I told him. "Dad," I said, "I think I saw Mom in a doorway, on my way to Pete's Miniature Golf with Erin." I had to tell him. Gosh, she lived a few miles away from our old house and had avoided us.

A romantic, my father asked a few typical questions a man in mourning might ask. "What was she wearing? How did she look?"

Pulling my mother by the arm, my father dragged her from the dirty area to the car. "We're going on vacation, to see someone. A specialist," he said. "You can forget about nursing, your children and anything else you want to forget about, but I can't forget about you." My father flung my mother over his shoulders. Jagged fingernails scratched his neck.

"Leave me alone!" My mother beat my father with her fists. "There's not a damn thing wrong with me! Let me go! Now!" Crazed eyes looked to people on the sidewalk for help.

Ignoring the vulgarity and stares, my father coolly excused the scene. "I'm her husband," he said. "She has amnesia."

Not one person tried to stop him. Can you blame anyone? The lady was insane!

My mother never drank liquor, but specialists dried her out in Canada. It took eight months, three days and several hours for my mother to completely recover from caffeine poisoning and return to her senses. After that, she warned us not to use caffeine. "Not one granule," she quietly insisted.

Bagging lunch, I'd rather be healthy than in a stupor. I'm me, and I'm happy.

Oh, I know why I lost focus in Mr. Moran's class. During lunch, Susan Ramsey put her Hi-Ho chocolate cake on my napkin. Not noticing chocolate specks on the napkin, I lifted my sandwich with the napkin. Chocolate entered my mouth, and I went into a fog, an attention deficit state.

Look around. Who have you lost? What does she drink?

24
Flowers for All Occasions

Photographer, Mike Dijital

Eight months and three days before Hurricane Alberto arrived, Amelia Baldwin misplaced her mind and priorities. Naturally quiet, Amelia became an outgoing woman, but she didn't know it. Unaware that something altered her, Mrs. Baldwin believed she maintained her natural, steady state.

Amelia's personality changes escalated during the trip to Happy-Land, an amusement park in Texas. The vacation turned out to be a downer after Justin chipped an upper on Mighty Mice bumper cars and Josh lost his lunch on the Caterpillar Crawler.

Except to stress Amelia and Brett, the getaway hadn't done a thing for the couple. Worse, Amelia discovered cappuccino, a drink that accelerated her altered, accelerated state.

"You don't need it," Brett said, pushing the stroller beside Amelia, as the all-American family sauntered to Coffee Emporium. "You had two cups of coffee this morning."

"My hands are sticky from cotton candy and wiping faces," Amelia responded, pulling up Josh's droopy shorts. "For crying out loud, one of them broke his tooth, and the other threw up. After this entire fiasco, I can treat myself to a cup of coffee!"

A cup of coffee turned out to be a sixteen-ounce jolt of cappuccino. One cup led to another.

Acting like amphetamine, cappuccino turned Amelia into a maniac for a few months, before two men injected her with pancuronium bromide and barbiturates, a drug combination that paralyzes and sedates, causing permanent sleep. That's right; caffeine instigated

Amelia's downfall, a jury found Amelia guilty, and she received the death penalty for, well, we'll get to that.

Two months to the day after sampling her first cappuccino, Amelia handed Brett a rolling suitcase. "Things haven't been the same since our vacation," she said, angrily. "Maybe you can stay at your brother's place for a week or two, while I clear my head." Appearing rational, Amelia panicked inside: *He's got to go! Are you doing the right thing? Of course, you are. You're perfectly sane. I had more fun at school, arranging gladiolas!*

"What's this about?" Brett asked, reluctant to pack. "We need to talk about this. Is there something you're not telling me?"

Rubbing her temples, Amelia claimed, "There's nothing to talk about. I'm burnt out and not happy with our marriage."

"I'm here for you," Brett said, kindly. "We can hire someone for the store." He attempted to hug his wife. Distant, she hollered, pulling away.

"We've had a bad year," Brett claimed, trying to console Amelia. "Things will get better."

"No, they won't!" Persuading Brett to leave, Amelia slapped his face.

As far as she knew, her situation would never get better. Thirty-two-year-old Amelia craved excitement. An outstanding journalist, an award winner, her husband bored her. The day to day of it, picking up the *Morning Glory* on the stoop, kissing the children on the forehead, petting their dog, and waving goodbye to Brett—previous enjoyments—repulsed her in her stimulated state.

Countless women would've gladly traded places with Amelia. And Amelia would have gladly traded places with herself—if she had known she was out of sorts.

Things had become routine. In between serving pancakes or chocolate flavored cereal, Amelia drank coffee, black with two sugars. Then she hurried her golden boys into the convertible and drove to Lambie Pie Nursery Care. Late to open Sunny Blooms, Amelia cruised through Cappuccino Charlie's and ordered coffee or cappuccino to go.

"Lady, are you sure?" a young waiter once shouted. "Maybe you meant a small cappuccino."

"Don't question me! I asked for a large, and make it fast!"

"Man, this chick is going to fly," the server remarked to a coworker. Filling a cup, he joked, "I'd hate to spend the day with her."

Flipping through the *Morning Glory*, Amelia drank, sitting in Cappuccino Charlie's parking lot, pondering. Fantasizing about the handsome man she met and how her life could change, Amelia didn't want to go anywhere or do anything. Then, after drinking the villain, she scanned her Timex and tossed the empty cup to the floor. Under the dash, the drink holder was too sticky for use. No need to discuss the stained carpet, but the carpenter is another story.

On a regular basis, Stone Ledin visited Sunny Blooms. "What's a nice girl like you doing selling flowers?" he asked, three days before Amelia vacationed with her family.

"I own the place," Amelia said, wrapping pink roses in glittered paper, "but sometimes I wonder the same thing."

The next afternoon, Stone handed Amelia a credit card for a plant. "Your job must be boring," he said. "I hope you get out for lunch or coffee during the day." And as Stone departed the store, he wished for fifteen minutes in bed with the cheerful saleswoman. Amelia focused on Stone's brawny back. A thought for a thought, some might say.

Home from vacation, Amelia felt like a new woman. Bony and pale, her nose a tad large, she removed her wedding band and slipped it into the nightstand. No reason to tell anyone I'm married, she thought.

Ah, Stone. The name's fitting for the rogue he turned out to be. But the neat haircut and starched jeans cloaked the man's negative traits, and his partner stood beside him through rain or shine. Frequently behind the ironing board, his overweight wife doted on the attractive cheater.

Denise never suspected that Stone lied and strayed. Discarding important information, coffee drinkers, Denise and Amelia evicted rational pieces from their heads.

What wouldn't make sense to strictly water drinkers seemed real in Amelia's mind, including Stone claiming he bought the dozen red Eleanor Roosevelt roses for his aunt in a nursing home. Stone didn't have an aunt.

It wasn't proper, but Amelia concentrated on the man, a carpenter six years younger than her. She couldn't stop herself. She sang, shucking corn, dusting the ivory elephant in the main hall, and in her head when making love to Brett. Obsessed, she tried shoving love lyrics aside, replacing sentimental songs with new age music, but love songs and thoughts of Stone squatted in her head. She escorted her delusions to the kitchen, bedroom, and into the garage.

Stone claimed he was single. "Happily free," he had said.

Amelia had no reason not to believe Stone—except he spent hundreds of dollars on flowers, girly flowers. In fact, Amelia believed the red roses were for Stone's sister. "Lynette is Ill with MS," Stone had said, several times. "I like to cheer her up."

I'm ill with MS, marriage syndrome, Amelia thought.

"Two sugars. The way you like it," Stone remarked, one morning. He handed Amelia a paper bag.

Seeing the cup of cappuccino, Amelia compared it with her diamond ring. "How thoughtful." *Yes, I will sleep with you! Marry you! Be with you always!* Amelia reached to stroke Stone's chin, and that's how the Baldwin nightmare began.

The following evening, Amelia lied, "Lois is going through a bad time. We're going to the movies."

"It's good you help your sister," Brett said, unaware that Lois encouraged Amelia to get psychiatric help, after witnessing Amelia's eyes caress Stone in Sunny Blooms.

Not amused, Lois had lectured, "I saw the way you look at him. If I didn't know you, I'd swear you were having an affair."

"Not yet," Amelia said, and grinned an imbecile's smile.

"'Not yet'? Don't tell me you're serious, because if you're thinking of ruining your life, you better get help, and fast. Happiness should be your six-room home, a husband who adores you and two toddler sons who need a stable mother. Happiness is not a Don Juan carpenter who's probably nailed half the women in town!"

"Get real," Amelia said, reaching for her cup of cappuccino. "Stay out of my business. Get real!"

"You said that. Now you're repeating yourself. That's so unlike you!"

It was not like Amelia to trade her husband for a carpenter, but that's what happened. Brett and Lois not knowing, Amelia cast Brett aside for Stone, meeting her lover at Willow's Way, a dirt lot near the railroad tracks. A few weeks later, she demanded Brett leave their home.

As for Stone? Two months after the affair started, he cast a fishing line at Porter's Peak, sporting with Roberta, a slender stenographer who wore tank tops above her belly button and thigh-high cut-offs.

"You were with the guys?" Amelia yelled, throwing a handful of fertilizer packets across the room.

"Lenny and the other guys asked me to tag along," Stone lied.

Calming down, Amelia reminded Stone that he had promised to call. All weekend she waited for a call. It never came.

"You don't own me, honey. I have a life, too."

What am I saying? I can't lose him. I have to handle this some other way. "What was I thinking? I'm sorry," Amelia said, rubbing the hair on Stone's fingers. "What about tonight? Come for dinner."

Justin and Josh threw potatoes at each other. Laughing about thick white clumps on their heads, Amelia tissued their faces. Angry without reason, Stone lectured about children behaving at dinner.

"They're just boys," Amelia said. Though insulted, she believed she was in love, and she didn't want to say too much to upset her man, not knowing her man shared himself with four women. "I'll see them to bed and put coffee on." *Because I'm so lonely. I'm lost without him here.*

With Amelia on the couch modeling a maroon nightgown, Stone mentioned leaving.

"But you just got here." *Don't go! I'll die without you here! Stay!* "Stay. Please." Amelia reached for Stone.

"You're pathetic," he said, heading for the door.

"Is there a problem?" Amelia asked, in Sunny Blooms.

"Alberto is due any day. I have a lot of work to do."

"Maybe you can stop by later. The boys will be in bed early."

"I don't think so. Not tonight."

Afraid to ask, yet more afraid to not ask, Amelia asked what the real problem was.

Stone claimed, "I don't like children but I love you."

He loves me! I knew it! "So what do you want me to do?"

"Find a nice guy to take care of all of you."

This can't be happening! You'll never be pretty, Amelia! Your sister is beautiful. You're smart. You'll have to use your brains! Mom, how can you say that to me? The truth hurts sometimes… Amelia, you'll learn! "But we can make things work, Stone. Please, give us a chance," Amelia pleaded for love from an indifferent liar.

After listening to Amelia make a fool of herself, Stone paid for a dozen scarlet roses. "Maybe I'll call you next week," he said.

A bat out of hell, Hurricane Alberto lifted roof shingles and brought down trees, porches and street poles. Many residents fled before the storm arrived, but Amelia sat in her sunroom, sipping joe, watching a stop sign spin, as if waiting for the metal to crash through the window and decapitate her. Thinking about Stone, Amelia almost ignored the telephone.

"The boys and I are safe. I made spaghetti, and we've been coloring. Are you okay?"

"I'm fine, Brett," Amelia dully responded, listening to wild rain and thunderous noises. "I'm just dandy." *Be careful, Amelia. Boys only want one thing!* "Thanks for calling."

"You don't sound convincing. Maybe we should get together for dinner tomorrow. I'll pay for a sitter."

"Not tomorrow, Brett"—*Get in this house, Amelia! Now!*—"I'm burnt out"—*You'll be the talk of the town! The talk of the town! The talk…*

The insurance adjuster handed Amelia his business card. "The tree came down and brought the deck with it. If I were you, I'd keep the slider closed." He touched Justin's baseball cap, snug on the little boy's head. "You wouldn't want anything happening to your children."

Who have you been with? Be careful, Amelia! They get what they want and leave you! "Thanks, I'll do that." *You'll learn! They leave you! Leave you, leave…*

Unkempt, resembling an abused rag doll, Amelia thought, They don't buy the cow when they get the milk…I don't like kids, no kids, won't have it, can't tolerate them…but I don't like kids! Brett wanted them! Hearing the screams, the mother covered her ears.

Elmo Fitzgibbon, owner of the ranch behind Amelia's house, had just finished changing a tire when he looked up and saw little limbs flailing. While he cut across back lawns, bloody water covered the boys.

The evening before, after spotting Stone entering the Peacock Paradise, a pickup bar, Amelia drove madly, almost knocking over a mailbox on the corner of Showboat Road and Pillsbury Lane. Swearing like a whore swindled of pay, she upset her boys.

After rushing the boys to bed, Amelia abandoned them, drove to the bar, looked for Stone, and ran to find his truck in the parking lot.

Disoriented, Amelia located her car, drove home frantically, dragged the kiddie pool where the deck belonged, and opened the slider.

After breakfast, with their mother senselessly grieving in another room, Justin and Joshua pedaled their tricycles across the kitchen floor, over the threshold, and fell to their deaths, landing in their turtle-shaped pool.

Attorney Piper asked, "Why did you allow your sons to die?"

Playing with snaps on her orange jumpsuit, Amelia said, "I didn't."

Wrestling the real with the unreal, Amelia couldn't provide a plausible answer for her actions because she did not believe she could ever put her sons in death's way. Baited by the surreal, the young mother knew she would never hurt anyone in her normal state, the healthy state she believed she existed in.

"Is Stone coming to see me?"

"Mrs. Baldwin, you shouldn't think about him," the lawyer advised.

"I know he'll be here. You'll see. He'll come to see me."

Under oath, Stone asserted, "I bought flowers in Sunny Blooms for my wife, Your Honor. Mrs. Baldwin and I had a strictly platonic relationship. She knew all along that I'm a happily married man."

115

25
Three Tickets Free

Dedicated to abused children

Toby hurried across the construction site, waving a newspaper. "Hey, Jake! Jake! Did you read the morning *World?* A guy named George Dickinson fell from the Ferris wheel at Yesteryear Amusement Park." Sweat ran into Toby's eyes. "You hear me?"

Reserved, Jake steadied a beam with his foot. "George Dickinson doesn't mean anything to me."

"But that's your last name, and it says here the guy's from Florida."

"Lots of people named Dickinson are from Florida." Pulling a nail from a stained pouch, Jake smiled. "I used to know someone named George Dickinson, but I don't. Not anymore."

"Don't screw with me. Are you related or not? Says here this guy 'has a rare blood type,' and the 'Blood Service Station Department put out a worldwide emergency search for compatible blood.'"

Jake shot three nails into the beam. "The first cut's the deepest. Remember that, and remember—I don't know George Dickinson." *Not anymore. And if George thinks my brother or I would actually donate blood if we could, he's out of his mind.* "Go back to work, Toby. We get paid to work."

Jake's father got paid to work, too. The city of Boston paid George handsomely to crawl into manholes. Callahan's Real Estate paid George well for selling houses. And George paid George well. Every Thursday afternoon, George cashed his paychecks, counted the money, and slipped half into a safe deposit vault. For thirty years, the father of three, George, did not send one penny for child support.

"I don't know when things fell apart," Harrison remarked. "He used to play doctor with us on the floor, with a plastic medical kit. He hung lights on the tree, and fed the rabbits. Remember the rabbits, Jake?"

Passing the hot pepper shaker, Jake mentioned the white rabbits, "He drowned them, Harrison. Remember we found him standing over the toilet, choking the little guys? We cried for hours."

Chewing onion pizza, staring at rowboats, Harrison wondered why their father murdered their rabbits. Next to him on the bench, Jake drank water, admiring rowers moving along the Charles River.

"You took a big fall, George." An elderly nurse pumped a rubber ball, taking George's blood pressure. Lorraine asked how he felt.

"Very weak."

"You'll be okay. Someone will come along with your blood type."

At the door, Sissy Sebastian snapped her fingers. Before speaking, she waited for Lorraine to fill in George's chart. "Why did you say that, Lorraine?" she asked. "You know how rare his blood is."

"He has children, and one of them is bound to be a match."

"What was he doing on a Ferris wheel at his age?" Sissy asked, rolling the medicine cart up the hall. "I'm half his age and won't go on one."

Bending to pick up a gum wrapper, Lorraine said, "A friend was in to see him, and said he's very active. He was up there looking for women."

In 1958, George married a good woman, an attractive one. But by the time Phoebe asked him to leave, he had broken her nose twice, using her as a punching bag, ruptured her spleen, jumping on her stomach, and caused a miscarriage, throwing her down the stairs. Phoebe had aged prematurely.

"What about the children?" Ready to burst into tears, George poured his third coffee of the day, repeating the question.

"We can share custody," Phoebe said. "They're your blood, too."

George put his head on the table. Ignoring apologies and pleas, Phoebe dried the breakfast dishes.

"Do you want the automobile, Mrs. Dickinson?" the judge clued Phoebe. She was entitled to their new car.

"No, Your Honor. George will need it to work. To provide for his children."

George provided for George. The Dickinson children, eight, six and five years old when George left, did not hear from their father again, but George heard from Phoebe and the children he deserted.

"I would like you to be an altar boy, Harrison," Phoebe said, straining pea soup. "After all, it's quite an honor, but I bought you shoes a few months ago, and sneakers for Christmas. I'm sorry, but I can't afford the black shoes the church requires."

Missing his father, Harrison asked if he could send him a letter. Phoebe didn't want her child to be disappointed, and she didn't want to be in the middle of a father-son relationship, the one Harrison believed he could have. She spelled George's address.

Harrison wrote a letter, the mailman delivered it, and George read and ignored it. Busy drinking imported coffee and packing for the

Bahamas, George looked forward to his five-day vacation, the Realtor of the Year Award.

"What a loser, huh, Jake? The guy couldn't call to say he loved us, or lie and say he couldn't afford a lousy pair of shoes. Luke and Alex laughed because I told them our mother couldn't afford the shoes. She worked so hard in the lamp factory. Her hands were calloused."

Harrison stopped going to church that year, 1972. Peeking through the peephole, watching Luke and Alex carry their robes up the street, Harrison thought, There isn't any God, because God couldn't be this cruel. A stable boy, who matured into a realist, Harrison eventually set aside most negative thoughts.

In the Intensive Care Unit, Lorraine fretted about possibly losing a patient. "Have his sons called?" she asked Nicole, a second shift charge nurse, ready to take over.

"Not that I'm aware of." Dumping used needles from a small container into a big, red one, Nicole asked the secretary if anyone called about Mr. Dickinson.

The Dickinson brothers skipped stones across the river. "What about my dinner?" Jake asked. "Do you remember the call?"

"Mom called him. She said, 'Jake would like you to accompany him to the Boy Scouts' dinner. It's a small affair, about thirty boys get together in the school cafeteria, to celebrate their merit badges.'"

Popping chocolate-covered peanuts into his mouth, as if essential to life, George had laughed. He said he couldn't make it. "To tell you the truth, Phoebe, I have my own life."

"You have children, George. You may want to remember that, because someday you might need them."

Holly needed her father before George needed his children. Tottering home from school during a blizzard, Holly met a sedan. It slid on ice, jumped the curb, and hit the young lady.

"Holly needs you, George. Your daughter was hit by a car, and she needs you." Phoebe squeezed the black telephone in the booth. "She needs blood, George. A nurse said that Holly's blood is rare."

"I don't know what to tell you," George offered, as a woman friend handed him his fifth cup of coffee of the day. "It's late, and I need rest."

"Please, at least let them test your blood. Please, George, I'm begging you. Holly's leg is shattered, and she has cuts all over her head. Her hair is sticky with blood, the needles are—Please!"

"I'm not feeling well myself." George tickled Verne's toes. "Let me call you back."

Beating her hands against the glass booth until they burned, Phoebe screamed.

Responding to an emergency call sent to every U. S. hospital, a field worker in Georgia donated two units of blood. A physician at the Blood Center advised Tucker against donating both units, but the man remarked, "It's only right. I hope someone does it for my daughter if she ever needs blood. Children are special people."

"What a man, Jake, a real man. Hell, our own father wouldn't even test his blood to help his daughter, and he wants our blood? He probably doesn't need blood. He needs black coffee shot through his veins," Harrison said, snapping a twig. "He drank it all day. Never water or milk. Just black coffee."

"I got sick on the smell when I was little, then I drank a cup at a high school event and threw up. That did it. You should see my coworkers, pumping the junk into their bodies. Half giddy, half crazed, some of them do a terrible job," Jake explained.

Nicole ran past the desk, shaking a bag. "Paige, a unit came from Texas! Mr. Dickinson is fading!"

Focused on sailboats waddling against the temperamental wind, the brothers thought about Freya. She made her uncles smile.

Dr. Hugo advised Holly against having the baby. "You have rare blood due to atypical antibodies. You may want to consider adopting."

I have a father who doesn't want me and a husband who adores me. "I'll make a terrific mother, Dr. Hugo. Joseph and I want our baby."

On July 3, 1989, Holly Westerly delivered a baby girl, and then she hemorrhaged. With every ounce of strength and courage, Holly held onto life. In the hall, Holly's husband, mother and brothers prayed she would survive. Their prayers failed.

Trying to stop the bleeding, forcing several towels against Holly, Dr. Hugo dislocated his finger. "Give her O Negative blood!" he screamed.

A nurse mopping Holly's forehead whispered, "Technicians cross matched them, but they're not compatible."

"I name her Freya," Holly sighed, closing her eyes for the last time.

"I feel great," Jake said, stretching his legs. "I'm going to call Joe tonight and invite Freya down. My wife and I would love to see her again."

"I was thinking the same thing." Harrison looked around for a trash barrel to dispose his water bottle. "I'll split the airfare with you."

"Someone better call a priest," Dr. Lafleur stated, switching off the light behind the bed. "We lost Mr. Dickinson."

119

26
Inclement Weather

Photo by J.M. Sawyer

Sharon Beals didn't expect to die. She wanted other people to die of embarrassment, but on the road of meddler's hell, trying to gain recognition and bring people down, Sharon Beals erred more than once.

Not much to look at, with her hair butchered to the neck and bulky thighs resembling cream cheese, Sharon, S to most, typed frantically. "How dare she do this to me!" she fumed, distraught that a newfound associate, best friend in Sharon's mind, moved forward, excluding nonproductive people from her life. *She dumped me! We were like school pals! How dare she!*

Drinking Hi-Test coffee and diet Captain Kid Cola, if there is such a thing as diet soda, Sharon stagnated in a delusional world, determined to get back at the woman for, well, for nothing. Had Sharon been able to accurately process information and not twirled in the imaginary place in her head, perhaps she would have comprehended the situation.

Happy with herself and her business, designing and selling nutritional dog food, Virginia Ellis did not ask for new friends, did not need them and did not want them. A diabetic, she worked from home, ran the treadmill at a health club, and diligently saved for her youngest son's college education. Before S entered her life, Virginia smiled a lot.

Obsessed with Damian's death, Sharon searched the Web for answers to her neighbor's loss. The seventeen-year-old boxer had died from "old age," a veterinarian told Bruce Hogan, but that answer did not satisfy Sharon. Preoccupied with finding another cause of the dog's death—one she could accept—S stumbled upon DogOrg-Food.vemt.

After reading about too much salt, the detriments of chemicals, and kidney failure in canines, S emailed the web site's owner, thanking Virginia. THANKS FOR YOUR GREAT WEB SITE! she wrote. IT'S

WONDERFUL! I LOST MY DOG TO KIDNEY FAILURE!

Virginia responded: You're welcome.

Persons diagnosed with schizophrenia tend to talk too much and cling to anyone that offers a sign of friendship, as trivial as the indication may be. And severely out of sorts, nearly drowning in her daily, three to six cups of coffee and six cans of colas, S fit the profile of a paranoid schizophrenic. Desperately wanting friends, wanting to connect with anyone that shared a pebble of interest in her, S emailed Virginia again, four times, sending links to sites about healthy dog food and causes of pet deterioration. Virginia responded to the second email. Thank you, she wrote. She deleted the mail without opening the links.

After S read *Tried and True Tricks to Healthy Pets* by Virginia Ellis, published online at *Dog Basket Magazine,* she wrote THIS IS WILD! GREAT WORK! YOU HAVE A GIFT WITH THE PEN! Out of town, visiting her mother, Virginia ignored her mail for a week. After reading S's letter, she deleted it.

Sharon did not get it. Courteous but cool, Virginia was not interested in developing a friendship with Sharon, a woman residing four states away. Concentrating on educating the public and controlling her diabetes, Virginia treasured the many friends in her life, individuals she counted on and vice versa, but for the next eight months S emailed Virginia. Juggling personal priorities, including spending time with her children and boyfriend, Virginia ignored S's letters.

Eleven months after sending the first email, S located Virginia's phone number and called her. The word horrific describes Virginia's view of the conversation. S spoke about experimenting with various spices and herbs, "to make a nutritional recipe for cats."

"That's a good idea," Virginia responded, when able to push a word into the one-sided conversation.

"But I don't know anything about recipes, and my friends who do are too busy to help me," S whined, trying to manipulate.

"That's too bad," Virginia replied.

"That's why I wanted to talk to you. You're very knowledgeable in this area. You really are gifted, you do know that, don't you? And you can help me!"

Virginia listened to the oven timer ring. "I really can't. I have too much going on, and I'm starting new projects," she said.

Obsessed with what she hoped to accomplish by feeding off Virginia and several other productive strangers, S experienced flight of ideas, rapidly moving from subject to subject. She told Virginia how her family abandoned her. "They can't stand me. They think I'm a basket case, you know. Ha! What do they know?" S mentioned being out of work. "Due to my inability to focus, I lost it, but everything will come back. I know it will. You'll see—everything will come back." She stated, "I need to help animals. It's not a want, that's my mission, like yours." Annoyed with S's rambling, Virginia concentrated on the chicken in her oven, hoping it didn't dry out.

Opening her fifth soda of the day, S asked Virginia what her plans were. "You know, for the future."

"I'm writing an article for *Days Go By Magazine*, and I may move to New York in the spring," Virginia replied. "Albany, to be near my cousins."

"Wow! '*Days Go By Magazine*'? That's a well-known publication. I'd love to work with the staff!"

"I'm not working with them. They want one of my articles."

"That's great!" S hollered. "You're going places!" *And I want to, too!*

The only place Virginia wanted to go was the dining room, to eat with Lucas and Mike. "Not really. I'm behind in my goals because my last worker erred, mixing up ingredients. I hired a new technician."

"What did you do to the person?" S asked, gleefully anticipating a story about Virginia getting back at the incompetent technician.

As if dropped from the sky, an omen swept over Virginia, an inner warning to detach from the strange woman. She asked what S meant.

"To get back at the person?" S asked. "What did you do?"

Searching for the gravy boat, Virginia said, "Oh, I'm not like that. I moved on with my life."

"Hell, you have more character than I do, because I would've got even with the person. There's always something you can do to make things right in your mind. You should have seen what I did to the last person that wronged me! I'm still making his life a living hell!" A shrill sound, a manic laugh, erupted from the psychotic woman. She picked up her Captain Kid Cola can.

Looking forward to hanging up, as S slugged cola, Virginia bowed out, "It's been nice talking with you, but I have to get dinner ready."

"I'll call you again! We can chat some more!"

The phone rang four times before Virginia realized it. Torn from her sleep, she wondered if someone had died. "Hello? Hello!" she groggily said. The caller had hung up. The phone rang again, but Virginia let the answering machine pick up.

"Hey, it's me!" S said to the machine. "I'm just calling to tell you…"

Seven eighteen in the morning. What normal person calls someone at 7:18 in the morning to chat? Most people are sleeping, eating bacon, showering or working at 7:18, but S was far from normal. Attempting to fill several voids, S wanted recognition.

"Hi, it's me, again," S said. "I caught something in our conversation and need to clarify. Do you have a minute?"

A minute, but not two hours. "What would you like to straighten out?"

"What did you mean when you said you want to head to New York? You need to move to my town, where we can get permits and open kennels for sick animals."

"Not this year, Sharon. I have too many things to do."

"What? What do you have to do? What's more important than helping animals? You have grown children. They don't need you." *I need you! Can't you see that? I don't have anyone, you selfish bitch!*

Virginia said, "I prefer maintaining a private life. Besides, I'm tired of putting together recipes. My family and I need a break."

"But your life belongs with sick animals, and I can get us funding. We'll open shelters and protect animals from abuse! That's what you want! It's what you strive for! We can do a lot, you and I can. I can call state agents and have them check places for us, places we can mix and cook pet food. I'm so excited about this! You should be, too!"

"Not this year," Virginia firmly stated. "My boyfriend and I are planting a garden, and I'm working on reversing my diabetes."

S seemed to relax. "Is that possible?" she asked. "How can diabetes go away? It's genetic."

Virginia maintained that diabetes stems from an altered physical state, not genes activated to change track mid-life.

"I hope you feel better." *Bitch!* "You deserve the best." *And so do I!*

"Thank you," Virginia said, fully meaning it.

Peace returned to Virginia. Not hearing from S for two days, she felt calmer and more together physically, but the "monsoon" approached. It arrived without warning.

"I contacted Professor Stamos, at the college near me, and I said you two should work together and study rosemary as a food additive. You two need to work together."

For more than half her life, Virginia coped with her father's and mother's controlling ways. An acquaintance from college controlled anyone she could, and her last boyfriend, an ex-Marine, demanded more attention than the average four-year-old. Familiar with the control web, Virginia knew S wanted to entangle her in the core.

I've got to tell her to go away, Virginia thought. S can't come into my life and try to control me. She's like a buoy around my neck.

Virginia emailed S, explaining that she did not need any help with her tasks, she had no intention of helping with projects, and she didn't need or appreciate anyone speaking for her. I hope we can move beyond this, she added. Please don't blow up the situation.

YOU BITCH! S wrote. AFTER ALL I DID FOR YOU! THIS IS THE THANKS I GET? GO TO HELL!

You took it wrong, Virginia wrote. I didn't mean to upset you. Call me, and we can talk about this.

Trapped in a dark, get-even world, S never called. Wanting to punish Virginia, she emailed nasty remarks, putting Virginia down. Hoping to discuss the issue rationally and move ahead, Virginia called S and left a message on her answering machine.

Fogged, her brain full of fluid, S put down the cola, and typed, I CAN SAY ANYTHING I WANT TO ANYONE I WANT! YOU ARE A BITCH AND I AM GOING TO TELL EVERYONE!

Opening the passenger door, Mike advised, "Virginia, you should stay away from people that contact you online. It's too bad you have to, but you can't trust everyone."

"I know I trusted her, honey, but she seemed nice."

Marlene said, "Hey Virginia, did you read the post at Betteranimals. vemt? Someone is degrading you and your articles published in *Pets For Us* magazine."

"Thanks for calling," Virginia said, turning on her computer.

Enemy to none, staring at vicious comments about her work and personality, well aware that S lacked common sense and had harassed other people, Virginia thought, S posted these negative remarks. No one else would've done this to me.

For months, well into the spring, almost every other day, S posted libelous comments. Due to the demeaning lies, Virginia removed her homepage and online articles. Without Virginia's articles, the world lost boxers, terriers, shepherds and other dogs.

"Why would anyone go to all the trouble to upset me?" Virginia asked, opening an aspirin bottle. "I didn't do anything."

"Sure you did, Virginia." Mike rubbed her shoulders. "You pissed the weirdo off because you have a brain." He asked if he should "take care of S," but Virginia didn't want anyone harmed. She wanted peace.

Gena stared at the online comments. "She's acting like a rejected lover, Virginia. You worked hard to get where you are. Real hard. The warped bitch probably saw your picture online and wanted you. When you told her to go away, she obviously lost it. That's so immature. So very childish."

With Virginia's glucose level rising and her appetite decreasing, Mike called a friend living eleven miles from S. "Hey, Stanley, do you know anything about a woman named Sharon Beals?"

"That miserable, overweight thing," Stan said, and laughed. "She's a horror show. How do you know her?"

"She's harassing Virginia."

"Tell Virginia to stay away from her. She's the talk of the town. My friend says she holes up in her apartment with the blinds drawn. Most of the time when I drive by the place all the lights are on, takeout lids litter the lawn and stuff's all over the porch. I hear the neighbors want her out of there."

Not normal according to her neighbors, Sharon perspired too much, trembled, staggered like a drunken soldier, panicked about the smallest situations, heard voices, misplaced items, forgot what people had said, and angered easily. Well over the line into schizophrenia-land, S coped with delusions, paranoia, anxiety, and auditory hallucinations. Ironically, or not so, given caffeine's ability to alter biochemical make-up, she believed she was fine. She had no idea caffeine changed her brain function many years before she discovered Virginia's web page. The sick woman had no idea she existed in her private disturbed world.

Stan said, "I talked to my friend, Mike. She harasses people. Like she gets her jollies out of it. One guy she followed got a restraining order on her. Then she targeted his neighbor. Nice kid, Francis Arbuckle. He never did a thing to anyone. I heard he was leaving the grocery store and didn't open the door for the psycho case, so Sharon attacked him personally. She smeared his name all over the Web, calling him everything from a momma's boy to a pervert. How normal is that? A good kid, he lost friends and a place on the basketball team."

"By the sounds of it, and considering what she's put Virginia through, the woman is trouble," Mike said.

"Man, she's more than trouble. She's sick in the head. You should see her." Stan lit a Marlboro. "The last time I drove by there I saw her on the porch, kicking a cat, swearing at the poor thing, and you say Virginia says Sharon 'wants to save abused animals'? The psycho lied."

Dottie Arbuckle, a tea lover, also lied. "I'm going out to get milk," she told her grandson. In bed, he moped. "Don't be sulking because some woman is telling lies about you online. We all know you're a good person. Hold your head high!" Traumatized, Franny shut off the TV, pulled a blanket over his head, and turned to the wall. Innocent, he wanted to evaporate.

Behind Cliff's Mall, wearing a long raincoat, her hair tucked under a hood decorated with sequins, Dottie spoke with Dino Fancy. "I don't understand why someone's harassing my Francis. A good boy, he doesn't need his name on the Web like toilet paper on someone's shoe."

"I understand your problem," Dino said, unhurriedly. He bit a cigar. "I can't say I need your money, Mrs. Arbuckle. I should almost pay you to have someone do it. The madcap lied about my pal's friend's sister-in-law online, almost bringing down her hair business. In a letter to *Our New Country's* editor, Sharon claimed the salon is infested with roaches. I can't make any promises, but I'll look into the matter."

Infected with poison dripping from her brain, down the back of her throat, into her chest, S typed. *He'll not make a fool of me! Al Sorenson, you'll be sorry! You'll fry in hell, you friggin bastard! Leslie Leminster, you'll get yours, too! Virginia Ellis, Days Gone By wants me! Franny Arbuckle, the door swings both ways, you momma's boy! Christa Iggly, you've not heard the last from me, you washed up figure skater! Dale, watch your cat... And all the rest of you! If any of you think you don't need me—you're wrong! Wrong! Do you hear me? Wrong, wrong, wrong!* Consumed, the pathetic woman never heard the front door close. She never spotted the dark-haired man dumping gasoline in her hallway.

In a casual, clandestine meeting at the local coffee shop, three town officials had agreed to look the other way if anything happened to Sharon Beals. "The entire town is fed up with the woman, Geoffrey," Mitchell Ruskin said. "We all agree that something's got to be done. Too bad someone doesn't just do her in." That's all Marvin, cleaning windows, needed to hear.

This isn't cool, Marvin thought, dropping a match, but like many town residents, he believed S deserved to be taken out.

"An eye for an eye," Dottie said, blessing herself in Dino's luxury Lincoln. "Thank you. The weight's lifted from my grandson's back."

Watching flames engulf the apartment building, Dino pulled a cigar from the glove compartment. "We both know it isn't Christian, Mrs. Arbuckle, to rejoice about a sad ending to a perverse woman." Dino grinned from cheek to cheek. "You don't have to thank me. This is a case of standing room only. My men and I never got the chance to discuss your problem."

27
Selective Serotonin Reuptake Instigators

Postcard, Weston State Hospital, Weston W. VA.
Courtesy of Blackwood Associates, Inc., Architects and Planners.

Fred and I occasionally argued, but we never hit each other or the children, so you may imagine how it shocked me when a policeman called my work to tell me our youngest was at the station. They arrested him for murder.

It all started three years ago, before we put Kenny away. Fred, Louise and I were watching *Forest Gump*, enjoying buttered popcorn and root beer, when Kenny fished the aquarium, grabbed Red, leader of the goldfish pack, and popped him into his mouth. "Kenny ate Red," Louise, too stunned to show emotion, said for us.

We were all shocked, but in our house life is less than a box of chocolates. It's a bag of soggy fries.

"Why did you do that, Kenny?" Pulling our son into the kitchen, Fred flaunted his anger, and I didn't blame him. "Why!"

Except to claim that Red threatened to jump out and strangle him, Kenny didn't supply a good answer. Fred sent him upstairs, and we tried focusing on the movie, but it was hard. Kenny had ruined the evening.

We should have replaced the fish and gone on with our lives, because Fred and Kenny would still be here. I'm telling you, these past few years crippled me emotionally.

By the way, I made coffee. All reporters seem to enjoy a nice, hot cup. Help yourself. The sugar is in that lobster-shaped bowl.

"He's got to go," Fred said, slapping the *Hometown Hornet* onto the table. "Miss Marshall said he has problems, and he's stressing us all, plain destroying our lives. He's got to go, Rose. Do you hear me? Last night—he ate a goldfish."

I wanted to keep Kenny home, to comfort him, to help him along. He was only fourteen. He didn't know much of anything. Goodness, they don't teach kids much nowadays. It's all rush, rush.

"Rose, I'm telling you," Fred threatened, "if you don't answer me and agree to observation, I will take him in. Think about it—He shot an elastic band at a classmate last month, earning a suspension, and you lost two days pay staying home with him."

They weren't bad days. I taught him to iron. I starched Fred's shirts, and ironing relaxes me. I thought Kenny may it enjoy it, but he scorched the cat. Eager to look out the windows, Licorice jumped onto the ironing board, and the next thing I knew, Kenny burned his tail. I'd rather forget it, but Licorice's scream sounded like someone was ciphering blood from old Mrs. Dupre, our neighbor behind us. The screech repeats in my head.

I flipped pancakes that morning. Chocolate chip. Kenny likes them.

Two days later, we signed him in, Fred and I. Dr. Littlefield said, "You're doing the right thing." Fred believed him, but I didn't. Kenny deserved a better place, better treatment for his condition.

"Kenny has bipolar disorder. I put him on a SSRI drug, similar to prozac and paxil," the doctor said. "It increases serotonin, a feel-good chemical. Let's see how he does."

Excuse me, but I must have a taste. Every day, I enjoy a few strong cups of the dark brew…Tastes good. Drink up.

I wanted to hang my head in shame. From a long line of strong people, I could never admit mental illness may run in my family. My relatives are workers, stable, strong. Uncle Melrose had a drinking problem, but he brought that on himself. That's not genetic. It can't be. It has to be learned behavior. Melrose grew up in a drinking family. He watched his father chase down the booze every night.

I used to believe that Kenny inherited his problems from his father's side. A doctor down south diagnosed Fred's sister Martha, the one who owns a bakery, with personality disorder. Now, I just don't know.

With Easter approaching, Dr. Littlefield agreed to send Kenny home. "He's doing well," the doctor said. "No significant mood swings. His laboratory results are a little elevated, but that's nothing to worry about."

Kenny fell behind in school. Miss Marshall assured, "He's a bright boy. He'll do fine."

Well, if "fine" is spending school vacation with crabs, then Gladys Marshall ought to redefine.

After we spent the day eating ham and chocolate bunnies at Ma and

Pa Hartland's house, Kenny decided to spend the evening with Terrence Sears, a musician's son. Kenny rarely went out at night, so his plans surprised me.

"Will Terry's parents be home?" I asked, concerned because Kenny seemed to have traded his good friends for riffraff.

Terrence had a bad reputation, and during Kenny's winter vacation, I found two empty nips in my son's parka, after he came home from the basketball game. He went with Terrence and a few other boys, the wrong crowd. I sat my son down, had a heart to heart talk with him about the dangers of alcohol and of becoming the company you keep. Kenny was always such a good boy, cheerful and smart. I didn't know why my son would lower himself, associating with a different element and experimenting with alcohol.

I never mentioned the incident to Fred, because our son seemed to understand what I taught him, and I never caught him with alcohol again or found any. Believe me, you, I searched his room and jacket.

Easter Sunday, shrugging his shoulders, Kenny assured us that Terrence's parents would be home, therefore Fred gave him permission to go out, but Kenny had lied. Mr. blow a trumpet and Mrs. hundred-dollar hairdo spent the week sipping coconut smoothies in St. Martin's, as their daughter supervised her brother. Lynne did a lousy job.

He was with a girl. Twenty years old, Lucy Moreland seduced my son on the back porch on a rusted couch swing that creaked. Busy entertaining the opposite sex in the upstairs bedrooms, Terrence and Lynne never heard them—frolicking like animals, no doubt.

As Kenny stood in the hall, scratching his private area, a blue paper slid from his jacket pocket. His brother, Tommy, my oldest, caught the condom wrapper before it dropped to the floor. That's how I learned about my son's evening.

Fred spooned sugar into his coffee cup and asked, "Did you take your SSRI?"

"What about the Crabkill?" I asked, rinsing the coffee pot before it stained.

Much is out of order here, as you can see. Books everywhere, coats on chairs. I grew up in a cluttered home, but I like to keep a few things in their places and looking new. The coffee pot is one of them.

Dull, watery eyes, once clear and the center of attention, ignored us. Kenny reached for the pill bottle. "This stuff makes me feel weird," he claimed.

"Take it," Fred ordered. "The doctor says it'll be a month or so before you stabilize."

"Yeah, but I don't feel right, like I'm not myself when I take this," Kenneth explained, bouncing a pill in his palm. We didn't listen.

"Swallowing a pet fish is not yourself," Fred said. "Take it."

Kenny washed the SSRI down with that Rocky High Cola, his favorite beverage. Many days, all Kenny drank was Rocky High. His Grandma Hartland started him on the stuff. She said it builds stamina.

Two months and three days after he began taking medication, Kenny lost his mind, not intact to begin with. Eating a goldfish is not normal.

A good boy, he got in trouble. A witness claimed he delivered the blow. "I saw the Hartland boy hanging out the passenger window, load a slingshot, aim, and fire. The bottle cap hit Mrs. Kneeland on the head, and she toppled over," a woman stated under oath.

Attorney Ludlow asked, "Miss Pals, how could you see all that when the car was moving?"

"I was moving, also," the high school dropout said, "pushing my son in his stroller."

Rena Pals didn't have a husband, just a son, so her judgment must've blurred somewhere along the line. I can't say for sure. I will say that Fred and I were blessed Dr. Hennigan took the stand. Jim Domino, our attorney, found Alvin Hennigan, a forensic psychiatrist.

Attorney Ludlow asked Dr. Hennigan if he thought Kenny's medication could cause psychosis.

"It depends," Dr. Hennigan coolly said, reaching for the courtesy glass of water. After a sip, he asked, "Does Kenny drink caffeinated beverages? Soda or coffee? Because most children ingest caffeine, and caffeine is a psychoactive substance. It acts like amphetamine."

Obviously annoyed, Attorney Ludlow leaned against the witness box. "Please, just answer the question, Dr. Hennigan."

"Yes, the SSRI could have caused Kenny to become psychotic," Dr. Hennigan stated. "SSRI drugs increase serotonin. Given Kenny's abnormal blood tests, the boy likely couldn't metabolize serotonin properly, or he had too much serotonin in his system. If he ingested caffeine, another drug that raises serotonin, Kenny could have become poisoned, which is a psychotic state." Next to me, Attorney Domino smirked, taking notes.

If you want more coffee, feel free. I store a few pounds in the basement freezer.

Assuming Bertha Kneeland would condemn our family, Fred and I held hands when she took the stand, but after Attorney Ludlow asked her a few questions, Bertha surprised us.

Ludlow asked, "Can you tell us what happened?"

"I was relaxing on my porch when I felt a sharp object hit my head," Bertha replied. "More stunned than anything, I fell. Slipping from my rocker, onto the deck, I broke my teeth, but the insurance company paid for new dentures, and it's about time. My teeth didn't break nearly as bad as when…"

"Enough in my courtroom!" Judge Barker banged the gavel.

"If Kenneth Hartland is found guilty, how would you like him punished?" Ludlow asked. The lawyer tapped his fingers on the bench.

Bertha answered, "To tell you the truth, your tapping upsets me more then the boy's actions. An old woman, I'm happy to be alive. I'd rather see children do something productive, like they behaved in the good, old days. I think adults should forbid children to eat junk food. Give them orange juice, apples, and peanuts, and put them to work helping old folks shovel snow, or make them paint a porch or two. You don't see that nowadays."

The judge sentenced Kenny to thirty-two weeks community service, and Fred and I discontinued giving our son the SSRI for a few weeks, but maybe the judge should've done something else, because things got worse. Sixteen days after stopping the SSRI, we told the doctor to put Kenny back on it. Maybe it was a mistake, but on a field trip to the Art Museum, Kenny paid eight dollars for a souvenir.

"What's going on with you, son?" Fred asked, raising the flowered ashtray. "You know your mother and I don't smoke!"

Jerking his legs, Kenny said, "I thought—"

"That's where you're wrong!" Fred fired. "You never thought! Lately you don't think!"

Drink up. The pot runneth over.

Usually I sided with Fred, but he went overboard. I wanted him to let up, but he kept insulting Kenny, and Kenny sat there, right over there in that plaid chair, taking it all in. I think he wanted to punch his father. I could see the rage build as he clenched his hands, but he sat, listening to Fred holler. Maybe I should've asked what was going on in his head. A mother is supposed to know what her child is thinking, but my son looked okay, younger even, like he hadn't aged in a few years. And the fish episode? I finally believed it Kenny's idea of a tasteless stunt, but I should've known something was wrong with him. I was always reprimanding him for something. "You wouldn't be doing this if your father were home," I constantly said.

For the most part, I raised Kenny on my own, but I raised him with values, morals, all around proper. I didn't raise my son to kill anyone.

We never knew about the gun. In a boot box, in the garage, he kept a pistol. With his schedule, Fred wouldn't have looked. He worked long hours, attended Lions Club meetings, and he liked the YMCA. I rarely went out there. Full of nails and tools, the garage is a man's place.

My boy called the station and turned himself in. "I don't feel like me anymore," Kenny said to the policeman cuffing him. "I don't know why I did it."

After leaving for school, Kenny came back to the house, grabbed the extra keys hanging in the kitchen, on the pineapple board, went into the garage and took the gun. Then he walked to the office building, opened his father's Lasabre, and crawled in the back. Hiding in the car, he waited for Fred. Several minutes later, on the freeway, Kenny jumped up, held the pistol to his father's neck and ordered him to drive to a wooded area. There, my boy triggered the gun.

It happened two years ago. Extremely remorseful, Kenneth really doesn't know why he killed his father. He knows their arguments had increased, but he knows that arguments aren't a reason to harm anyone.

I don't know what possessed Kenny to do it, but he's my son, and I will stand by him. That's a mother's duty.

Kenny says he's feeling a little like his old self again, and he seems to be doing okay at the hospital, but maybe it's me. Nearly at the end of my rope, I miss Fred terribly, I no longer remember what Kenny's normal state is like, and sometimes I question my own.

Attorney Domino helped me. He managed to have my son moved from prison to the state hospital, and he found a new psychiatrist. Attorney Domino and Dr. Phillips agree—Kenny does not belong in a locked cell. He's just a boy, a teenager. He's not Clyde Barrow.

Safe in the institute, my son waits for the trial. I sent along some Cadoo chocolate bars and Choco-Bites, because I know how Kenny enjoys his sweets.

"There's a case before the Supreme Court, Mrs. Hartland," Dr. Phillips said, leaning back in his leather chair. "Every day, for several months, a teenager ingested a SSRI drug with Captain Kid Cola. One evening, he stabbed his grandmother while she slept. The lady never gained consciousness. I do believe we have a similar situation."

Dr. Phillips showed me the book that mentions caffeine inhibits monoamine oxidase. It was written in 1967. He said any drug that inhibits monoamine oxidase can cause attention deficits, mental illness, and much more, and that type of drug should never be taken with a selective serotonin reuptake inhibitor because the combination of the two may cause craziness, attention problems, and suicide, but why isn't it public knowledge that caffeine inhibits monoamine oxidase? Why can't Louise find the information on the Web?

The doctor knows best, but I'm not sure I want to believe that caffeine or the combination of an SSRI drug and caffeine harm people. After all, everyone ingests caffeine. The people in charge of food safety wouldn't let us down. Could they?

Before Fred's death, I assumed our son's mental illness might stem from Fred's side of the family, but now I wonder if something happened in the world to cause millions of people to be diagnosed with mental illness. What could've happened to so many people?

Drink up. The sugar's in the lobster-shaped bowl. Help yourself.

* * *

About Mike "Dijital" Turcotte, Photographer

Since 1998, Mike "Dijital" Turcotte has been a photographer. Most notably known for his extensive photographic documentation of the Danvers State Hospital and other prominent abandonments throughout Northeast America, Mike organized Operation Tiptoe, an event where donated flowers were planted next to forgotten, nameless gravestones at the Danvers State Hospital.

Mike's photographs are featured in Michael Ramseur's book *Haunted Palace: Danvers Asylum as Art and History*. Mike and his photography have also been featured on the Hallmark Channel's "A New Morning."

Mike is considered one of the grandfathers of Urban Exploration and one of the most recognized names in the Urban Exploration, Extreme Photography community.

To view Mike's work, see www.dijitalphotography.com.

About Ruth Whalen

Allergic to caffeine and misdiagnosed for most of her life, Ruth Whalen recovered from brain poisoning several years ago, researched, and wrote. Her articles about caffeine allergy and caffeine psychosis, published in the Journal of Orthomolecular Medicine, Medical Veritas, Positive Health magazine, online at www.doctoryourself.com, and in other print and online publications, and her book, *Welcome to the Dance: Caffeine Allergy, A Masked Cerebral Allergy and Progressive Toxic Dementia*, are helping people recover from "mental illness," progressively deteriorating physical conditions.

A writer and medical technologist, able to think out of the box, Ruth is on a mission to save the children from caffeine, undereducated doctors, a lifetime of "mental illness" and psychiatric drugs. She knows that people may disagree with her findings because many people do not understand chemistry and immunology. However, the show must go on to help people recover and regain their natural states.

A free spirit, Ruth resides in a small, New England town. She is writing another book.

CPSIA information can be obtained at www.ICGtesting.com
Printed in the USA
LVOW101615111112

306825LV00002B/180/A